THE JAZZ FLOWER

THE JAZZ FLOWER

A NOVEL

Vee Williams Garcia

iUniverse, Inc.

New York Lincoln Shanghai

THE JAZZ FLOWER
A NOVEL

iUniverse books may be ordered through booksellers or by contacting:

iUniverse
2021 Pine Lake Road, Suite 100
Lincoln, NE 68512
www.iuniverse.com
1-800-Authors (1-800-288-4677)

This novel is a work of fiction. Any references to real persons, events, establishments, organizations, or locales are intended only to give the fiction a sense of reality and authenticity. Other names, characters, and incidents are either the product of the author's imagination or are used fictitiously, as are those fictionalized events and incidents.

ISBN-13: 978-0-595-38174-6 (pbk)
ISBN-13: 978-0-595-82541-7 (ebk)
ISBN-10: 0-595-38174-X (pbk)
ISBN-10: 0-595-82541-9 (ebk)

Printed in the United States of America

PROLOGUE

▼

New York City
January 1951

He had threatened her before but never hit her. This night was different. Outraged by her insults and actions, he backhanded her face, hurling her to the floor. She lay still, appearing unconscious. Her eyes ballooned. Tears rushed down her cheeks, evidencing her pain. The fusion of his citrus cologne and natural musk assaulted her nostrils. In a moment, a few of her fingers flexed. Her arms and legs moved a little. It was apparent she was regaining her senses and strength and would momentarily rise from the carpet.

Diving to the floor, he over-reached for her and merely grazed one of her arms. Quickly realizing again what was happening, she cried out and scrambled away from him, across the carpet to the desk. Straining her arm, she grabbed a leg of the leather armchair at the desk and pulled her body up high enough to let her free hand reach for something. Her fingers discerned a tray filled with pencils, pens, and possibly a letter opener. She then felt and latched onto what she knew would serve her best. Wrapping her fingers around the scissors, she yanked them from the desk a split second before he grabbed her foot and clutched her ankle.

With greater control of her, he gripped the back of her leg, between the knee and thigh.

She clung to the sturdy chair leg with one hand and to the scissors with the other. Then, stabbing backwards blindly and fiercely, she lacerated something.

He jerked away from her, cursing as he saw rich red blood from the gash in his hand spurting everywhere.

Shoeless, and with her sweater and torn skirt splattered with his blood, she quickly pulled herself up with the help of the desk leg. Still gripping the scissors, she lunged, stabbing him in the face, neck, chest, anywhere and everywhere until he lost his ability to fight back or even keep his eyes open. Holding his head he fell to his knees, then slumped to the floor and lay still, breathing laboriously.

She looked down at his motionless bleeding flesh, then bent down and retrieved her purse from the floor near his body. Purse in one hand, she gently touched her bruised, aching face with the other. She moved towards a chest of drawers with a large mirror above it, and inspected the damage he had done to the side of her face. Then, with a handkerchief from her purse she walked around the room and wiped off seemingly every surface her hands had touched.

Afterwards, she retrieved the bloody scissors from the floor, took them to the bathroom, and washed and dried them with a towel. Giving the instrument that saved her life a final once-over from tip to handles, she held the scissors within her handkerchief and returned them to the desk tray.

She found her shoes and slipped them back on her feet. She then pulled his jacket from the chair it lay across and slid her arms into its sleeves. It hung on her like a coat and hid her torn blood stained clothing well. Pulling the coat-like jacket around herself, she opened the door and left, found an exit at the rear of the building, and slipped into the wintry night.

PART I

CHAPTER 1

▼

Washington, D.C.
Autumn 1949

Early on a November morning, the bare-branched trees along Summit Place were bleak and unwelcoming. Possessing a haunting look, their mood seemed gray like the skies and as grim as the cement sidewalks across which insects and other tiny creatures scurried. No humans walked on the sidewalks yet. No cars moved along the street, which was lined on either side with Victorian Style row houses. The facades of the narrow three-story homes offered no clue to the sort of people who lived within them.

Inside Number 13, a red brick house with gray trim, Rosa Stills was in her bedroom, preparing for her travel to New York City. With only a flimsy white slip, bra and panties covering her shapely mocha-hued body, she fastened the large tan suitcase sitting on her bed.

In the suitcase were underwear, a robe and slippers, a couple of dresses, skirts and blouses. She had thrown in a couple of sweaters and two pairs of shoes. Rosa promised herself she would buy more clothes, stylish ones, once she started making money in New York.

After setting her luggage on the floor, Rosa sat on the blue quilt covering her bed and slipped her feet into a pair of black shoes. Her nostrils flared at the mingled aromas of freshly made coffee and fried bacon and eggs wafting from the kitchen, all the way upstairs to her second floor bedroom near the back of the house.

With her shoes on, Rosa sat up and was aware of her chest expanding as she inhaled the savory breakfast smells. "Um-m-m," she uttered. After standing to pull on a cream colored blouse and navy blue suit, she touched her ears to be sure both small silvery earrings were fastened properly. Then while surveying her appearance in the mirror above her dresser, she mused about the nightclub job in New York City that she was going to start and its importance to her jazz singing career. She applied red lipstick to her lips, pressed them together, and double checked in the mirror to be sure the lipstick was on neatly. Rosa then gathered everything she needed to take downstairs.

Black, crimpy hair framed her face and bounced on her shoulders as she headed out of her bedroom and down the hall towards the stairs. With a tweed coat over her arm, a black pocketbook in one hand and her suitcase in the other, Rosa was about to walk downstairs, when she heard a terrified voice coming from the first floor.

"Rosa! Rosa! Call Dr. Peterson! Call Dr. Peterson!" shouted the high-pitched voice.

Rosa dropped everything, ran down the stairs and, following the sound of the voice, rushed into the dining room.

"What's wrong? What's wrong?" she asked, assuming her mother's loud voice and alarming tone.

Nora Stills' naturally honey yellow-skinned face was drained of color. Her slender middle-aged form cloaked in a pink robe was kneeling on the floor, as she held her own mother's light-skinned wrist. "Your grandmother's fainted," she said, her hands trembling. "I can barely feel her pulse."

Rosa looked from her kneeling mother to her gray-haired grandmother, Lilly, lying in a blue housecoat on the dark wood floor.

"Rosa, call Dr. Peterson!" Nora shouted again.

Rosa kept staring down at Grandma Lilly, whose normally pink skin was now ashen.

"Call him! Now!" Nora screamed directly in Rosa's face.

Rosa jumped and raced from the dining room, across a brief hall, to the living room, grabbed the telephone, and quickly dialed a number.

After making the call, she rejoined her mother, who was still kneeling on the dining room floor. Nora was solemn as she told Rosa that Grandma Lilly collapsed after leaving the breakfast table.

While they stayed close to Lilly's still form and waited for the doctor to arrive, Rosa was thinking: *Please, God. Please let Grandma Lilly be all right. Don't let her die and keep me from going to New York today. Don't let her delay me from living my dream the way she's always tried to do.*

Rosa's eyes glazed over as her mind's eye brought back her early childhood years—years she had occasionally revisited by listening to her parents' stories and frequently through her own memories.

Rosa's memory had stored the hurt she felt upon first realizing that Grandma Lilly favored her brother and sister over her. And Rosa's mind refused to forget how Grandma Lilly's apparent contempt of her through the years had threatened to destroy much more than Rosa's self-esteem.

CHAPTER 2

▼

Washington, D.C.
1930

By the time Rosa was a toddler, the United States had entered the difficult economic period called the Great Depression. People all over were feeling the dire effects of the Depression, but it did not appear to affect Rosa's D.C. family. Her parents, Douglas and Nora Stills, were an elevator operator and a visual artist, and her grandparents, William and Lilly Johnson, were a lawyer and retired school teacher. From outward appearances they seemed wealthy. The truth was they lived with the motto, *Waste not, want not,* and were in the habit of holding funds in reserve for hard times. Douglas was originally from a Chicago family of the working poor, and fortunately he managed money well.

The abundant attention Rosa received from both sides of the family from her birth in 1927 through her toddler years did not spoil her. It served only to make her feel special. However, when Rosa was between three and four years old, her Grandmother Lilly began withdrawing the attention she had once shown little Rosa, and hence dampened the special feeling Rosa had previously enjoyed.

To Rosa's dismay, Grandma Lilly stopped holding her as much as she used to and ceased showing Rosa the affection to which she had become accustomed. Now, whenever Rosa ran behind her grandmother, trying to attract her attention, trying to grab hold of her skirt or apron as she did so, Grandma Lilly would not slow down. Instead Lilly would walk faster, causing little Rosa to stumble and fall to the floor. Unhurt, Rosa would scramble to her feet and chase behind Grandma Lilly again. Lilly kept moving briskly around the kitchen, or whatever room they happened to be in, going about her cooking or whatever she was engaged in at the time.

Sometimes when Lilly was sitting in a chair in the living room, reading a magazine or listening to the radio, Rosa in her childish playfulness would start climbing into her lap. Lilly would shift her knees, causing Rosa to fall to the side. Or she would actually push Rosa away, saying, "Grandmother's reading now dear." At times she would tell Rosa, "Run along and get your toys, dear. Grandmother's listening to an important radio program right now."

"I want to sit on your lap, Grandma", Rosa would persist.

"Call me Grand*mother*, not Grand*ma*, Lilly would reply in a sharp tone. "I've had to tell you that too many times, Rosa. Now I want you to remember it."

Though Rosa felt like crying, she would hold her trembling lips together firmly, trying not to let the tears spill over her eyelids. Then she would leave the room, find her toys and play with them for a long while. Playing with her toys for a length of time made Rosa forget her Grandmother's strange treatment of her for a while, the same way that Christmas Time would help the whole family forget how mean Lilly could treat them during the year.

From around the first week of December through New Year's Day, when Rosa's parents undressed the tree and took it down, Lilly was nothing short of pleasant. The Christmas Season was her favorite time of year. She became the picture of benevolence, giving gifts to everyone in the family on Christmas morning and to relatives and friends who visited later in the day. She in turn received many gifts.

Lilly made sure Christmas in the Johnson, Stills home was generously displayed and full of happiness and joy. She and Nora decorated the halls with holly and the entrances to the living room, dining room, and kitchen with silvery garlands. To the glittering entryway frames, they attached colorful Christmas cards that streamed into the house from friends and family throughout the Holiday Season.

During the Holidays, little Rosa felt like everyone in the house gave her extra love, like creamy confection spooned onto a dessert.

Early on Christmas morning, Rosa would run down the oak staircase to the first floor hall, make a sharp right and skip into the living room. With sparkling eyes she would open her presents. While she was playing with her toys, her parents and grandparents would come downstairs, gather around the tree, and exchange the gifts they had purchased and carefully wrapped.

In mid-morning, Grandma Lilly would cook a country breakfast for the family. After they finished eating, the women washed the dishes and cleaned the kitchen. Nora then assisted Lilly in preparing the turkey, ham and the remainder of Christmas dinner.

Later in the day, the two women set some of the platters and bowls of food on the old oak wood buffet that sat alongside a wall in the dining room. And they placed much of the food, including the turkey, on the long lace-covered dining room table.

In late afternoon—early evening, family and other relatives, and a few invited friends sat around the table and listened to Grandpa William bless the food. Then everyone enjoyed Christmas dinner. Afterwards, all through the evening they felt welcome to return to the table and the buffet to refill themselves.

All during the Holidays joy floated through the house; while sacred and popular Christmas songs and carols played on the record player and radio. Such magnification of the season and unbridled celebration left no room for Grandma Lilly's pre-Christmas snide remarks and demeaning behavior.

Promptly after New Year's Day, however, Lilly returned to her usual self. And little Rosa felt the sting of rejection and lack of affection from her all over again. In her own mind Rosa couldn't understand why Grandma Lilly changed towards her. Everybody else loved her. Why had her grandmother, who had once extended the most open welcoming arms, the broadest lap on which to sit, and the most comforting bosom against which to snuggle, stopped liking her? Why did the person who had at one time seemed most protective and most accommodating suddenly cast her aside as if she were a raggedy doll or an ugly old toy? These were questions to which Rosa needed answers. But even in her child's mind she was not yet ready to ask anyone in her family the questions. Instead she learned through experience not to seek Grandma Lilly's affection. And she began trying to regard her grandmother as just another person, like a visitor who was temporarily staying at the house.

CHAPTER 3

▼

Rosa was in kindergarten when her brother Willie was born a week before Thanksgiving Day, in 1932. It was the same month in which Franklin D. Roosevelt was elected United States President, ending Herbert Hoover's gloomy time in office.

In Roosevelt, the country had a brand new president who inherited the Great Depression. President Roosevelt promised and looked forward to instituting social programs, or a New Deal. And the Johnson, Stills family had a new baby, a boy whose birth promised the continuation of their name and bloodline.

Douglas was so happy to have a son that he telephoned his parents in Chicago about fifteen minutes after the baby was born—much sooner than he had notified them of Rosa's birth.

He and Nora named the baby William, after Rosa's grandfather, because Nora wanted it that way. Douglas did not mind. After all he had his son. They nicknamed the baby Willie to differentiate between grandfather and grandson.

Over the months, Willie's skin changed from the pinkish color of an infant to a doe-colored hue. The hint of keenness in his facial features suggested that he would eventually resemble his mother and maternal grandparents; much to grandmother Lilly's delight.

Douglas was ecstatic to have a son to carry on his name, and he talked much to Nora about how he wanted to raise little Willie. "I want my son *and* my daughter, to be down to earth like my side of the family," he told her. "And I'm going to do all I can to make sure it happens."

With a new baby in the house, Rosa realized she no longer received most of the family's attention. They now showered their affection on baby Willie. Because of that, Rosa began showing off, trying to win a slice of the attention and affection her parents and grandparents doted on Willie.

Rosa danced around the house and sang from the time the sun came up in the morning until it was time for her to go to sleep at night. She crooned songs she made up as well as tunes she heard on the radio. Rosa memorized songs recorded by Louis Armstrong, such as *Memories of You, Stardust,* and *When You're Smiling.* She sang them often, even when she happened to be present during the grown-ups' important discussions. When Rosa was that interruptive, the adults shushed her. After realizing her performances gained her some attention, she focused on learning new songs and improving her dance steps. At her discretion, she showcased her routines in front of the family to garner coveted attention and approval. She built a small repertoire and a real act to show off to relatives who visited on holidays. Soon her desire to perform caused her to dream of little else. Little Rosa often declared, "One day I'm going to be the best singer in the world!"

CHAPTER 4

▼

In June 1934, when Rosa was seven years old and Willie only two, their baby sister was born. The birth of a third child was an exciting event in the Johnson, Stills world. Happenings in the outside world that year also excited the family.

Major national events engaged them in exciting discussions. They talked about Arthur Mitchell of Illinois becoming the first Colored Democrat elected to the U.S. Congress. Nora and Douglas talked about Zora Neale Hurston's *Jonah's Gourd Vine* and Langston Hughes's *Ways of White Folks* being published. Nora and Lilly were delighted when Sculptor Augusta Savage became the first Colored member of the National Association of Women Painters and Sculptors.

Grandfather William was most excited about Arthur Mitchell's success and about his own work as a civil rights attorney.

*   *   *   *

Rosa and Willie's tiny sister entered the world on a mild, sunny day in June. Red and pink roses, yellow chrysanthemums, and other flowers were in bloom. Trees flaunted bright green leaves. Grass was verdant and lush. A dewy freshness was in the air.

During the full beauty and ripeness of springtime, the infant emerged from Nora's womb prematurely, weighing only five and a half pounds. Nora named the baby Dorothy and nicknamed her Dot, saying she was as tiny as a dot at birth compared to Rosa and Willie. Rosa had come into the world at seven pounds, three ounces. And Willie had weighed in at eight pounds, sixteen ounces.

Right away, Grandma Lilly did everything for infant Dot, including bottle feeding her, changing her diapers, dressing her for bed at night, and singing to her. When Dot became a toddler, Lilly read stories to her at bedtime, something she never did for Willie or Rosa. Lilly made dresses for Dot and always combed Dot's light brown hair. She showered attention and affection on Dot so much that it seemed Dot was Lilly's child instead of Nora's. But Nora didn't seem to mind.

With Lilly relieving a third of the stress of motherhood from her, Nora began to focus more on Willie. Douglas, proud father of a son as he was, also centered much attention on Willie.

With so much of the family's attention focused on Willie and Dot, Rosa began to feel grossly neglected. She acted out her feelings by bossing Willie. With little provocation, she began pushing him and hitting him. One day, her grandmother caught her bullying Willie and spanked Rosa's hand and sent her to her room.

Whereas Willie acted adoring of baby Dot, Rosa was distant and never tried to help her mother or grandmother do anything for the little one. More than once Nora, Douglas, and Lilly caught Rosa pinching the baby. Douglas reprimanded her, becoming sterner with each occurrence of her negative behavior against Willie or baby Dot. Nora and Lilly would spank Rosa, telling her she was the oldest child and they wanted her to help take care of Willie and Dot, not bully or hurt them.

In spite of Rosa's bossing Willie and occasionally mistreating him, Willie retained a happy-go-lucky personality and played games with Rosa whenever she was in the mood to play with him. He never harbored anger. He was more often mischievous in a merry way, and his brown eyes twinkled when he was up to something. Although he could entertain himself with his own toys, he chose more often to socialize with Rosa, his parents, and Grandpa William, whenever they showed their willingness to play with him. He learned his grandmother was not playful at all. And he saw that she focused most of her attention on Dot.

Realizing she had lost her throne as the favored child, Rosa began engrossing herself in her own world of music and song. From the time she was seven years old until she was ten, Rosa learned songs she heard on the radio. The popular Fats Waller song, *Ain't Misbehavin*, and a special number, *Black and Blue,* featured in the Broadway Musical, *Hot Chocolates,* were Rosa's signature songs for a while. Rosa was oblivious to the true meaning of the adult theme of *Black and*

Blue, which concerned a dark-skinned woman's complaint about her man's preference for lighter skinned rivals. However, little Rosa sang it like she understood it, even at her tender age.

Nora was not amused by Rosa's preoccupation with songs like *Black and Blue* and *Ain't Misbehav*in'. She voiced her concern to Douglas, saying, "Rosa is way too young to be singing about being faithful and saving all her love for one man—for a man, period. We probably shouldn't be letting her listen to the radio so much, Douglas."

"I don't see anything wrong with it," Douglas said. "Besides, singing gives her something to do that she really likes. It seems to make her feel good about herself."

Rosa's grandmother scorned the idea of Rosa learning jazz at all, branding it as music and songs created by low class people.

Nevertheless, Douglas let his mother-in-law know he approved of Rosa shaping herself into an entertainer, and he encouraged Rosa to continue learning and singing songs she heard on the radio. He just didn't see how it could hurt her, he told Lilly.

"Besides," he emphasized to Nora, "a lot of the songs Rosa is learning are blues and jazz numbers from my Chicago roots. And don't forget blues and jazz were created from Colored people's experiences. Remember how much fun you and I, and Henri and Lenore had listening to jazz in those nightclubs in Paris years ago? It hasn't been *that* long ago, Nora, now c'mon."

"Yes, I remember," Nora said, chuckling.

"Okay, then why shouldn't Rosa learn and sing that kind of music? Why shouldn't she love it? Nora, you've got to admit you can see talent oozing out of her. I just think we should nourish her talent, that's all."

After listening to the strong case Douglas presented, Nora agreed to continue letting Rosa learn songs from the radio. She also agreed with Douglas that in a few more years they could start letting Rosa listen to recordings from his prized jazz collection. "Maybe we can let her take piano lessons too," Nora added.

*   *   *   *

At John F. Cook Elementary School, several blocks away from Summit Place, Rosa proved to be a quick learner. She loved learning and was an excellent student. She excelled in reading, writing, science, and arithmetic. And of course she did well in creative activities such as play acting and singing.

Rosa was full of energy and loved to socialize. She liked the other children, but she bossed her classmates when they let her. After one incident in which she forced a classmate to do something against his will and then saw him complain to the teacher, Rosa backed off. The one thing she did not want was her teacher's disapproval. When she proved herself to be the smartest student in class, she also wanted the teacher to recognize her as the best-behaved student. Then her grandmother would hear about it. Grandma Lilly would be pleased and begin to love her again, Rosa mused.

At home Rosa became well trained in the amenities. She learned to be polite and to respect her parents and other grown people. Grandma Lilly was the main grown-up who instilled those behavioral attitudes in Rosa, since Nora was occupied with her art career, and Douglas and William were away from home working much of the time.

Nora was teaching art at Howard University again and also busy with her own paintings; so it was Lilly who had the time to teach Rosa to walk and sit like a lady, to smile and be pleasant in her conversations, to be demure. She stressed the importance of these behaviors to Rosa. Hence Rosa couldn't ignore her grandmother's presence.

Lilly also instilled in little Rosa that since she was dark-skinned, she should be careful not to do things that made her stand out in a bad way in a crowd. In that way, she said, Rosa would have a better chance of being accepted in society. She would be welcomed into the best circles. The idea of Rosa's dark skin being something that was not good was an idea Lilly suggested to Rosa frequently.

This thing of being accepted was mysterious, as Rosa thought that almost everyone in her family loved her and did not treat her differently from the way they treated people with lighter skin. Only Grandma Lilly brought up this thing about Rosa's color.

Rosa thought she knew what circles meant. She and her friends played games in which they formed circles, in the classroom and on the playground. But what was this thing about society? It seemed to be some far away place where only hateful people lived. Rosa decided to question her grandmother about society.

Lilly responded, "Society is a world of important educated people, who are mostly light-skinned and good looking. People in society have lots of money and own beautiful things."

Rosa didn't understand her grandmother's definition at all. In her prayers at night, Rosa prayed that someday she would be light-skinned, so her grandmother would love her as much as Mama and Papa loved her.

Although little Rosa loved her grandmother and desired her love and approval in all things, deep down inside herself, she feared she would never receive it. More than once she asked her mother about it. On one occasion, she ran down the basement steps and found Nora in her art studio.

"Mama, does Grandma Lilly love me?" Rosa asked.

"Of course she loves you, sweetheart, now run along and play. Mama's working on a painting right now. And I've got to finish it soon, okay?"

"Okay, Mama," Rosa answered. But she felt her mother's answer did not make her feel better or understand Grandma Lilly's behavior towards her any more than she did before."

When Rosa asked her father, "Papa, does Grandma Lilly love me?" she received a different kind of response.

Douglas answered her question with two questions. "Why do you ask me that, baby?" He bent down and scooped her into his arms and then stood up, holding her. "Did she say she didn't love you?" he asked Rosa, with a cloud over his face.

"No, Papa," Rosa answered. "Grandma Lilly said if I don't do things right, people will notice my dark skin more and they won't like me. And she said if I don't walk and sit prop-er-ly, I won't be accepted in society. Papa, what is society?"

The cloud over Douglas's face darkened. "Don't you worry about understanding society. Grandma Lilly's society is just a bunch of silly people. You're a smart girl. You look just like your mother. And that means you are very, very pretty."

"But Mama's skin is not dark like mine."

"That's all right. You still look like her and you're just as pretty. You'll always be Daddy's pretty girl. You don't ever have to worry about that stupid society, all right, sweetheart?" he smiled, kissing her on her cheek. He then let her down, allowing her to stand on the floor. "Now, I want you to go upstairs to your room and pull out some paper and crayons. Draw some pretty pictures and color them for me. After that, I want you to stay in your room and practice your songs for a while, okay, my precious flower?"

"Okay, Papa," Rosa said, grinning as she bounded up the stairs.

Rosa loved her father and mother. But her father held a bigger place in her heart. He always took time to explain things to her in a way no one else did. He always tried to make things right for her, and that made her feel special. However, even though he helped her feel better about that place called society, and he let her know she would not be missing anything if the people there did not like her; Rosa still wondered if she would ever receive Grandma Lilly's love and approval.

Rosa feared that, though she knelt and closed her eyes extra tight every night and prayed for it, she would never be light-skinned.

Douglas strode from the brief hallway, into the dining room and back to the kitchen. There he found Lilly cooking. "Mother Lilly, I don't care what you do in your own life. I don't care what you say to Nora, because Nora is a grown woman. She thinks like a woman and can answer for herself—"

—"Douglas, what on earth are you getting at? What are you talking about, dear. I *am* trying to cook dinner here. Please get to the point."

"The point is: As long as my family and I are living in this house, as long as I and my daughter have breath, don't you EVER say anything to Rosa that makes her feel less than the beautiful, intelligent child that she is."

"Douglas, what *do* you mean?"

Douglas's frown grew more pronounced. He took a deep breath and turned away from Lilly a moment. And then, still angry but appearing to be in control, he answered her.

"I *mean* that mess you told her about being good so people won't notice she's dark-skinned. I *mean* that garbage you told her about sitting and walking right, so she can be accepted into your so called high society."

"I don't like your tone of voice, Douglas. Remember, I am your elder. I am your mother-in-law. You need to show me respect."

"Yeah, well, when you stop talking to my daughter as if she's not worthy, I will give you some respect. She's just a little girl. She doesn't understand all that stuff you're telling her. And even if she were older, I would not want you talking down to her like that. Papa William doesn't do it. You shouldn't either. You're her grandmother, for God's sake. Show her some love!"

"Douglas, teaching her the right way to act to become a proper young lady *is* showing her love, whether you realize it or not."

"Do me a favor will you, Mother Lilly? Save it 'til Rosa's old enough to understand things for herself and decide whether she even wants to be in your type of society. And something tells me she won't. Number one, because she's my child. Number two, because Nora and I are *not* raising her to be snobbish."

"Really, Douglas. Someday you'll thank me for trying to teach Rosa the things she needs to know to get along in this world and make the right choices in life."

Frowning deeper, Douglas glared at Lilly. "Oh, I see. You want her to make better choices than Nora did," he said, his voice rising. "You'll probably want Rosa to marry some light-skinned college educated man. Is that what you're driving at here? Nora made the wrong choice in a husband. So you have some twisted idea that you can mold Rosa to succeed where Nora failed? Why don't you just come out and say it!" he shouted.

Turning raspberry red, Lilly stuttered, "Well—well—I...I never said that, Douglas. I—I—uh—"

Without a word, Douglas stormed out of the kitchen.

CHAPTER 5

▼

1937

Rosa was in fifth grade when she started piano lessons on Saturday mornings, several blocks from home. Douglas agreed with Nora that he should accompany Rosa to her lessons. Although Rosa was ten, she was not old enough, they concurred, to travel to and from her lessons alone.

Sometimes Douglas drove Rosa to her lessons in the family's black Ford sedan. But often they walked. He waited for Rosa until she finished her lesson and then walked back home with her. Rosa enjoyed their walks. They allowed her to talk to her father freely about the music they both loved and to share with him her dreams for the future. She talked with him about her love of swing and jazz more comfortably than she did with anyone else.

Nora seemed pleased that Douglas was bonding in this way with Rosa. Apparently Nora wanted Rosa to have as good a relationship with Douglas as she had had with her own father while she was growing up. And Douglas's time with Rosa allowed Nora more solitary time in her studio, to work on her paintings.

After one of her piano lessons, Rosa was enjoying her walk with her father as usual. Her hair was in two braids and she had on a yellow check dress, white socks, and black shoes. Douglas moved easy in a white shirt, brown slacks and brown shoes. The two strolled, sometimes chatting, sometimes not. Their silences were easy as they moved along, nearing their house on Summit Place. Douglas was content in his role as husband and father. Rosa was happy fulfilling her love of music and felt fortunate to have the best father in the world. But after they arrived home, something happened that destroyed their good mood.

As they entered the house and headed through the hallway, they glanced to their right, into the living room, where Lilly was sitting in one of the burgundy-colored wingback chairs near the fireplace. A gold-colored floor lamp was next to her chair. She held open a women's magazine and seemed to be engrossed in whatever article she was reading. Her once black hair was now streaked with gray and hung loosely on her shoulders. And she appeared comfortable in her pink housecoat and slippers.

At Lilly's feet, sitting on the dark brown hardwood floor was little Dot. Dot was in a long-sleeved white nightgown with tiny yellow flowers, playing quietly with her dolls and other toys. A second chair, like the one in which Lilly sat, stood at the other side of the fireplace. The matching burgundy-colored sofa was against the adjacent wall alongside the windows. Dusty rose-hued drapes at the windows complemented the furniture.

Lilly peered over the top edge of her open magazine and looked at Rosa and Douglas before they passed the living room. Without greeting them, she blurted, "Douglas, Nora tells me you're taking Rosa for piano lessons." Her tone was clipped. And her light skin turned red as it always did when she was about to make a passionate point or insult someone. "I hope she's learning classical and sacred music and not that trash you and Nora let her listen to on the radio."

Snatched from their pleasant, peaceful time together, Douglas and Rosa stopped in their tracks. Rosa winced at Grandma Lilly's tone and comment, and then looked at her father, hoping he'd say something appropriate and save them both from further attack.

Douglas took Rosa's hand, leading her into the living room with him. He smiled and winked at Rosa, as he gently let go of her hand, saying, "baby, go on upstairs and tell your mother what you learned at your music lesson with Mrs. Gibson this morning."

"Okay, Papa," Rosa said, gratefully exiting the scene she felt was about to intensify. Once out of the living room, Rosa ran up the stairs.

Douglas turned back to his mother-in-law. "Mother Lilly," he began, "Rosa is just learning the basics right now, okay? But down the road, after she's learned how to really play music, she can make her own decision as to what kind she wants to play."

"What do children know?" Lilly retorted, laying her magazine on her lap and giving her undivided attention to Douglas. "They must be taught," she said. "They must be guided and directed."

"Yes, but in a positive way," Douglas said, his voice rising. "Not in a negative, destructive way."

Rosa stood at the top of the winding stairs, listening to her father and grandmother talk. She had heard them in that same line of argument many times.

Hearing them now somehow reminded her of her family's past summer vacations on Martha's Vineyard, in Massachusetts. While other children played at the beach on the Vineyard and were in the sun all day, Grandma Lilly cautioned Rosa, Willie, and Dot. She told Willie and Dot to stay out of the sun, so they would not become dark-skinned. But with Rosa she modified her caution to include the admonition, "…so you won't become even darker than you are." At the end of a sunny day on the Vineyard—and sometimes in their D.C. home as well—Grandma Lilly would bathe Rosa with milk and lemon juice and rub her little knees and elbows with half a lemon, trying to lighten them. She never treated Dot that way. Dot seemed as if she would forever be her Grandmother Lilly's favorite grandchild.

After they returned home to D.C., Rosa mentioned to her mother that Grandma Lilly had bathed her with milk and lemon so she would become light-skinned one day. Nora simply told Rosa the milk and lemon would not hurt her, and that she would always be her same beautiful color. Rosa felt better since her mother called her beautiful. However, when Nora related the story to Douglas later while they were alone in their bedroom, Douglas was furious to hear Lilly had treated Rosa that way; especially after he had asked Lilly firmly not to do it any more. He told Nora they should definitely get their own place and move out of Lilly's house; because Lilly was never going to change. He didn't want Lilly causing his daughter to feel inferior, he re-iterated.

Nora persuaded Douglas that as long as they said and did things to instill confidence in Rosa, they could override anything negative Lilly might say to the child. And she argued that they should continue living with her parents in order to save money and not have to worry about child care, while they worked or were otherwise away from home. She said that in the long run, Rosa would have a stronger sense of family if she continued living with her grandparents as well as her parents. Douglas calmed down, but said at some point he was going to have a talk with Lilly again, and he was going to tell her if she could not give positive direction to Rosa, then she should leave Rosa's rearing totally to him and Nora.

*   *   *   *

On a daily basis, when Rosa became too imposing by showing off in order to get attention, her grandmother said cruel things to her. She said, "Now, dear, you already draw attention to yourself the minute you enter a room, because of your color. Don't make things worse by singing those crass songs and doing those primitive dances you do. I don't know where you learned those kinds of songs and dances anyway."

Rosa began something new: defending herself. "Grandma, you don't know about me! I learned my songs from the radio, and I'm going to sing them in front of a lot of people one day. I'm going to be the best jazz singer in the world, you'll see."

Nevertheless, since Lilly often attacked the thing that Rosa loved most—her jazz singing—Rosa feared she would never receive what she desperately wanted: her grandmother Lilly's full love and approval.

As usual, when Douglas heard Lilly voicing negative thoughts to Rosa, an argument between him and Lilly ensued. And all the old discomfort Douglas had suffered by not being accepted by Lilly and her elitist relatives and friends, when he first came to D.C. as Nora's husband, were brought to the surface again.

Lilly won their arguments by simply talking over Douglas in quiet tones and cleverly brushing him off. She then justified her color-conscious statements to Nora and Rosa by saying she was preparing Rosa for the way the child would be regarded and spoken to in the outside world. And if Rosa wanted to have the slightest chance of being accepted in the outside world, she should be more reserved and let her education and culture speak for her, not her outlandish behavior, which only drew attention to her dark skin. Those kinds of statements always hurt Rosa, but she grew to the point where she just shrugged them off or pretended for a while that Grandma Lilly didn't exist.

But during the times when Lilly was unavoidably present, Rosa resumed wondering why, if her parents could encourage her to feel equal to anyone else, her grandmother could not. With her grandmother, Rosa's color always got in the way, and it made Rosa feel her grandmother was never going to love her. Although Rosa was not able to totally break the grandmother-granddaughter bond that had been formed while Rosa was a baby and a toddler, she did halt outward display of affection for Lilly. And Rosa chose to be in her presence only at family meal times and other occasions when it was impossible to avoid it.

After hearing enough of her father's and Grandmother's angry words, Rosa moved from the top of the stairs. She padded into her parent's room to tell her mother how her piano lesson had gone, as Douglas told her to do.

Douglas was still arguing with Lilly. "Yeah, well…I think children need to be taught good values, and they need to be directed towards behaving well," he said.

"But as far as what they like and dislike culturally, I think they can decide for themselves—that is as long as they're not hurting anyone in the process."

"Humpf," Lilly grumbled, shrugging her shoulders and turning her attention away from Douglas and towards little Dot.

Little Dot was holding up one of her dolls for Lilly to see. "Grandmother, Grandmother, look! Look!" she said.

"Yes, my darling, I see! Now dress another doll as well as you did that one."

"Okay, Grandmother," Dot chirped, returning her attention to her dolls and fabrics.

Lilly didn't look at Douglas again, but picked up the magazine she'd been perusing when he entered the house, and resumed her reading, obviously dismissing him.

Douglas shook his head and started walking up the stairs to his and Nora's bedroom. It was obvious to him Lilly wanted each of her granddaughters to develop in a way that would ensure they would marry someone in their own class, someone whom Lilly thought would be better than he was. He knew that although Lilly had reluctantly accepted her only child's choice for a mate, she still did not approve of him. He also knew from over hearing conversations between Lilly and Nora, that Lilly wanted Nora to push Douglas to seek training that would put him on the road to what Lilly considered a suitable career path, at least to a better position than what he already had—an elevator operator's job at the Stanton Hotel.

Lilly was obviously frustrated that Douglas's job didn't matter to Nora. But Nora did not care about Lilly's frustration. What made Nora happy was that Douglas was a good man and a faithful husband. She did not care that he was not a college graduate. He was a better person than most college graduates she knew. And she did not need for Douglas to make more money.

Nora had her teaching salary from Howard University. Also, through her connections at Howard, Fisk, and Columbia Universities, and with the help of her white friends, Nora's still life paintings, landscapes, and portraits were selling well. They were selling not only to colleges, but also to privately owned galleries in D.C., and to museums in various states around the Country. Therefore it didn't matter to her that Douglas worked as an elevator operator and, of his own initiative, brought in extra money by cleaning offices at the Negro law firm where his father-in-law worked. Nora and Douglas never argued over money or whose earnings supported their family most.

*   *   *   *

Rosa was determined not to let Grandma Lilly stop her from going her own way. She focused on becoming important, on becoming the best singer possible, and on achieving what she wanted. She wanted two things: to become a great jazz vocalist and to make the person of her dreams—the person she loved most outside her family—her own. That person was Alan Covington, a boy in her Sunday school class whom she had latched onto when she turned ten years old.

Alan Covington was the lightest, handsomest, smartest boy she had ever seen. He paid attention to her like none of the other boys or girls did. With him, her dark skin did not seem to matter. Alan said.and did things that made her laugh, and he showed he enjoyed being near her. Rosa felt wonderful in his presence, as if being near him satisfied some deep need. When she was around him, she felt as beautiful as the light-skinned girls were said to be, and she felt totally accepted into society.

When Rosa was eleven, she had a memorable encounter with Alan. One afternoon during a children's choir rehearsal at their church, Rosa was on her way to the bathroom and ran smack into Alan in the hall. He had just left the boys bathroom and was on his way back to the social hall. They apologized to each other and in doing so, their faces brushed. They hesitated. Alan turned red. Rosa could feel her heart beat wildly against her chest. Their eyes locked for a moment. Without thinking, Rosa kissed him quickly. Rather than pull away, he lingered, holding onto her and their kiss. They heard footsteps entering the hallway, and only then did they pull apart. Alan went back to the social hall, and Rosa, smiling and feeling a sense of accomplishment proceeded to the girls' bathroom.

They were the only ones who ever knew about that kiss. And while Alan re-entered the social hall as Iris Haywood's boyfriend, Rosa knew she had something from him to hold in her heart. The fact that they kissed the way they did let her know her color did not matter to at least one person in her peer group—the most important person, as a matter of fact; for she'd had a crush on Alan Covington for a long time. And that kiss he gave her strengthened her hope of one day loving someone like him; it let her know she was totally accepted by an important light-skinned person other than her mother.

CHAPTER 6

▼

1940

Over the months, Nora and Douglas observed Rosa's seriousness at studying her music lessons. When she turned thirteen years old they bought a small piano for her. They had the deliverymen place the black musical instrument in the living room.

Whoever sat at the piano could then see the sofa along the wall to their left. The narrow vertical windows above the sofa were still graced by dusty rose-colored drapes. An end table with a lamp on it was at one end of the sofa. Directly across the room from the piano was the fireplace. Burgundy-hued wingback chairs were still placed, one each, on either side of the fireplace. A gold-colored floor lamp stood beside one chair, and a small table with a regular lamp stood beside the other chair.

Having a piano at home helped Rosa as she progressed in her lessons to more complicated songs.

Soon Mrs. Gibson wanted Rosa to study voice as well as piano. However, Rosa boldly told Mrs. Gibson that since she felt confident enough in her natural ability to sing, she needed to study only the piano, not voice.

Mrs. Gibson disagreed. She was of the opinion that classical training in voice could help any singer. But Rosa stood her ground and insisted she did not want to waste her parents' money by taking voice lessons when she did not need or want them.

Nonetheless, Mrs. Gibson was like Rosa's grandmother in that she tried to discourage Rosa from focusing on singing jazz songs. She persisted in talking to Rosa about becoming a classical singer instead. Rosa would develop into an excellent contralto, Mrs. Gibson insisted.

"Why you could become another Marian Anderson. She's a great singer. Didn't you read or hear about her drawing a crowd of 75,000 colored and white people when she sang at the Lincoln Memorial last year?"

"Yes, Ma'am, I did." Rosa answered. "And I don't want to disrespect you, Mrs. Gibson, but if I'm going to see anyone in concert, I want it to be a jazz singer; because that's the kind of professional I'm going to become."

Mrs. Gibson's matronly mushroom-colored face flushed red. She shrugged and cleared her throat. "Well, young lady, let's get started with today's lesson."

Rosa made it her business to learn a few sacred and classical songs, and a few Negro Spirituals. She didn't learn them to please her grandmother Lilly. She had given up on that. And she did not do it to please Mrs. Gibson. Rather, she did it because she knew that that knowledge would serve her well whenever she was in a church play or other program. Looking far ahead, she intended to impress the church members and other associates who might one day become jazz fans of hers and one day pay to see her perform.

Douglas continually encouraged Rosa, and he let her listen to blues and jazz recordings, some of which he had purchased, and others that his friends and family in Chicago and Kansas City had mailed to him. Rosa listened to the recordings on Douglas's and Nora's record player. She listened as well to the radio, to musicians like Count Basie and his orchestra. That listening exposed her to Basie's signature piece, *One O'clock Jump,* and other numbers he made famous with his orchestra and with singers like Billy Holiday. Basie had hired Billie Holiday in 1937—the same year Ella Fitzgerald, at age 19, had become known as the First Lady of Swing. Rosa listened to Duke Ellington's *It Don't Mean a Thing If It Ain't Got That Swing* and she paid attention to *Stompin' at the Savoy,* and other popular dance numbers.

As Rosa developed her repertoire, she added some of her favorite Duke Ellington and Count Basie compositions to it.

In school, whenever she was called to perform in a play or talent show, she was ready and willing. And if the teacher didn't stipulate the kind of song or music that should be performed, Rosa invariably chose a jazz number.

When she was in junior high school, she sang the song A *Stairway To The Stars* as a solo act in a couple of programs. Dressed in a long blue dress and white socks for one of those programs, she sat at the piano on stage and began playing the music. Then she began to sing softly, "Let's build a stairway to the stars…and climb that stairway to the stars". Building slowly and projecting her voice to the audience, she continued, "with love beside us to fill…the night with a song."

She looked at the audience as if to say, *I am somebody special. Come with me on my journey and witness me becoming a star.*

When Rosa was halfway through the song, she rose from the piano bench, walked to the microphone at center stage and resumed singing to the accompaniment of one of her classmates, who had slipped onto the piano bench the moment she had risen from it.

Her voice was full and rich for a young teenager's, and as she closed her eyes and crooned the remainder of the song, she exhibited the confidence of a professional chanteuse and an interpretation that was beyond her years. After the program, she received mixed reviews from her family.

"Your song was wonderful, baby," her father said.

"Thank you, Papa. One day I'm going to be a professional," she blurted with joy in her voice.

"Your performance was really good, my love," Nora told her.

"Thanks, Mama."

"You sound just like those singers on the radio," Willie said.

"Well, thanks, little brother," Rosa responded.

"Rosa, you sing good," was five-year-old Dot's comment.

Rosa bent down and picked up little Dot. "Thanks Dot," she said, squeezing her.

Grandma Lilly said, "You may have sung well, Rosa, but that kind of music and low class singing style won't get you anywhere in life. You ought to study classical music and voice. With classical training, you'll be able to teach voice, once you get your degree, and—"

—"Quiet, Lilly," William snapped. The child did well." He then turned to Rosa. "You've got real talent, young lady," he said.

"Thank you, Grandpa," Rosa said gratefully, feeling he saved her from Lilly's intent to steal the glitter from her special night.

CHAPTER 7

▼

Washington, D.C.
1949

It took Dr. Peterson only eight or ten minutes to drive to their house. But to Rosa and her mother, the wait for him to arrive seemed like hours. Rosa was still praying for her grandmother to be okay; so she could go to New York as scheduled and start her new singing job there.

A middle-aged balding Doctor Peterson, in a brown suit and carrying a small black bag, bent down and touched Lilly's throat. He lifted her wrist and held it between his thumb and forefingers. He then gently laid down her wrist. His look told Nora and Rosa there was no pulse. Lilly was gone. With a solemn face, the doctor pronounced her dead. "Probably caused by a heart attack," the doctor mumbled, knowing Lilly's medical history. "An autopsy can be done to establish the precise cause of death. Do you want to have an autopsy done?" he asked Nora.

Solemnly, Nora shook her head in the affirmative.

"All right," Dr. Peterson said. "I'll call for an ambulance to take her body to Freedmen's hospital. The autopsy will be performed there." Having paid enough social and professional visits to the Johnson, Stills home, Dr. Peterson knew where the telephone was. He retrieved the extension in the living room and phoned the hospital.

"Oh, my God," Nora said quietly, her hand moving from her forehead backwards through gray-streaked dark brown hair, to the back of her neck. She held her hand there for a moment, while breathing in and exhaling bullet breaths. She sat slowly into a chair, slumped back, let her limp arms rest on the arms of the chair and, with her face towards the ceiling, closed her eyes.

Rosa, still standing and looking somber, said flatly, "It's just like Grandma Lilly to die when I'm on my way to New York to *really* start my singing career. She always was good at putting a damper on my dreams."

Nora's strained face twisted to red distortion. She rose slowly from her chair, walked with deliberateness over to Rosa, and slapped her daughter's face with a force that swiveled it from one side of her neck to the other.

Rosa's hand flew to her face, covering the skin where Nora's blow inflicted a stinging bruise. Tears welled in Rosa's eyes, and she trembled, fearing Nora might hit her again. She had never seen her mother so angry. Holding her face with both hands, as tears streamed down her cheeks, Rosa said in a quivering voice, "I'm sorry, Mama. I'm sorry. That just came out. I didn't mean to hurt you. I didn't mean to hurt you, Mama."

Without saying a word or acknowledging Rosa's apology, Nora, pale and expressionless, turned and walked back to her chair and sat down.

As if he hadn't witnessed their exchange, Doctor Peterson asked Nora, "Which funeral home should pick up the body from the hospital?"

"Winston's," Nora said curtly, without moving.

He made the call for her.

After speaking with Winston's Funeral Home, Dr. Peterson phoned William at his law office and told him to come home right away. Choosing not to tell William over the phone that Lilly was dead, Dr. Peterson said only that it was a family emergency and William should drive home right away.

Rosa postponed her trip to New York and helped Nora with the obituary and funeral arrangements. She telephoned her agent, informed him of her grandmother's death, and told him that she would have to postpone starting the New York nightclub job until she felt comfortable about leaving her family.

After disconnecting from her agent, Rosa climbed the stairs, returned to her room and her bed. Her resentment at her grandmother's timing to die gnawed at her, forcing her thoughts back…back…back…

CHAPTER 8

▼

Washington, D.C.
1940

Because Rosa desired to impress her teachers and appease her grandmother, she joined her junior high school choir and was often chosen to do solo parts when the choir performed.

She became more familiar with a few choir members who were in a couple of her regular classes. One of them was Elsie Taylor, a quiet caramel-colored girl of medium height and weight. While Rosa was in the choir to please her teacher and her grandmother, as well as to strengthen herself as a performer, Elsie was in the choir simply to gain an extra credit.

Elsie was not a soloist and was content to remain in the background as one of the choir's numerous alto voices. She initiated the first conversation between herself and Rosa. It was after a rehearsal in which Mrs. Powell, the music teacher, selected Rosa to do a solo in a special program.

"Hi, Rosa, aren't you in my English class?" Elsie asked.

"Yeah, I am," Rosa answered.

"I thought so," said Elsie. "You know, you're definitely the best person for that solo." Elsie was obviously excited. "You're so talented!"

"Thanks," Rosa said, smiling. It was not often that students and other people were as open and kind to her as Elsie was. Rosa didn't want to lose that. "What are you doing after school?" she asked.

"The usual. I'm going home, eat a sandwich, and start my homework," Elsie replied.

"Why don't you come to my house? We can do our homework together, and after that I can play the piano. I'll show you some of the songs I've learned from radio," Rosa said.

"Okay. That sounds like fun. Where do you live?" Elsie asked.

"On Summit Place, Number 13," Rosa replied.

"That's right around the corner from my house." Elsie seemed excited at the discovery. "Okay, so when I get home from school, I have to let my sister know where I'm going, and then I'll come over to your house."

"All right, see you then," Rosa said. She too was excited but refrained from showing it.

Rosa and Elsie became best friends. They were seen chatting and laughing together between classes and after school. Gossiping on the telephone about teachers and students they knew became a favorite source of entertainment for them. They also enjoyed talking about Rosa's dreams of becoming a world-class jazz singer and musician.

Elsie was the same height and nearly the same size as Rosa, but not quite as bosomy. Rosa gave Elsie clothes she no longer wanted. Elsie wore the second hand dresses, skirts, blouses, and jackets proudly and seemed to value them as perks of her friendship with Rosa.

Elsie was a follower and not especially creative. But she was a good listener. Rosa valued Elsie's skill at listening as much as she valued her ability to keep their secrets.

CHAPTER 9

▼

Washington, D.C.
1942

The United States was entrenched in World War II. It had involved itself in the War after the Japanese bombed Pearl Harbor, in Hawaii, around nine months before Rosa started high school.

When Rosa enrolled at Dunbar High in the fall of '42, she was already known by some students for her talent and aggressive personality. Many of Rosa's classmates did not like her, but she did not care. She walked tall at school with her head up high. She appeared aloof to most of her schoolmates. The only time Rosa seemed warm was in her music classes and while she was on stage performing. Elsie, whom Rosa regarded as a true friend, was enough for her. But if she did not have even one real friend she'd be okay, she told herself. She'd always have her most prized friend—her dream of becoming a renowned jazz singer—to keep her company day and night.

At Dunbar, Rosa chose extra-curricular activities which she thought would help prepare her to become a professional. Another way that she prepared herself was by listening to her father talk about the new sound created by Kansas City musicians and how Count Basie and his orchestra had a great rhythm section and that Basie was hiring talented singers. Her father's knowledge of the jazz scenes in Kansas City, Chicago, and New York, intrigued her. And it inspired her to practice her singing and piano-playing extra hard.

And Rosa joined the Dunbar High School Choir and performed solos during concerts. Whenever there was a talent show, she participated by singing songs that Ella Fitzgerald and Billy Holiday made famous. She always won starring roles in school plays. But she often had to demand to do an audition for a major role, which she knew she could play better than another girl who was favored for the part. When she was not selected even then, she would sabotage the girl who was chosen.

One day before a performance, just as a chosen actress walked past her down the hall, Rosa stuck out her foot, causing the girl to fall, injure her leg and be forced out of the show. Rosa then, fully knowing the girl's songs and lines, volunteered to replace her in the show. Above the fallen girl's protests, Rosa ended up being the star of the show and saving the production.

As she grew older, Rosa noticed that her staunchest competition was a group of girls who were three or four shades lighter than she was. Ranging from olive-complexioned to cream-colored with a tinge of pink, they turned red when they blushed, or were angered or embarrassed. Possessing mostly light brown, straight to wavy or curly hair and keen features, their bodies varied from feminine and willowy to athletic and big-boned. Everything about Rosa's voluptuous body was in contrast to theirs.

From head to toe she looked different. Where their facial features were definitely keen, Rosa's nose, though straight, was rounded at the tip, and her nostrils barely escaped flaring. Her black hair was crimpy. It was neither course nor soft but she was challenged to tame it, especially during warm humid weather. She brushed her mane a lot and wore it in large braids on either side, or sometimes she pulled the braids up and across her head and secured them with hairpins. Other times she pulled her loose hair back and bound it with a colorful ribbon or with decorative combs on either side. Rosa was about five-feet, seven and curvy: full breasts, a narrow waist, full hips and derrière. Her legs were long and shapely. Clearly she did not possess the look of a wispy debutante.

There were times when Rosa wished she was less full, but it didn't bother her enough to tear at her self-esteem. She realized her body shape was more like the relatives on her father's side of the family. Rosa loved his down-to-earth people, whom she'd gotten to know during her nuclear family's visits to Chicago.

The one thing Rosa always felt was a shortcoming was the dark color of her skin. Her grandmother had made sure of that. Mentally, Rosa fought against letting her skin color make her feel inferior or less worthy of affection or attention than her lighter-skinned siblings and schoolmates.

Fortunately, Elsie always served as a buffer for Rosa. Elsie was light brown enough to be accepted by many of their very light-skinned peers. The ones who did accept Elsie, and talked easily to her, provided her with news and gossip which she shared with Rosa. It did not matter therefore that the very light-skinned girls turned a cold shoulder to Rosa. Through Elsie, she was privy to their information anyway.

CHAPTER 10

▼

At age 17, Rosa's coffee-with-chocolate skin color was flawless. Her figure was full and shapely. She was outgoing on the one hand but aloof to cold on the other. When opportunity allowed, she employed her wit and used cutting remarks to humiliate her lighter skinned girl classmates in front of each other and in front of the boys. Rosa called those girls high yellow witches. They called her "black Rosa."

Iris Haywood, who had been going with Alan Covington for quite a while, especially disliked Rosa. It was general knowledge between Iris and her cronies that Alan turned red and became fidgety whenever Rosa was present. Alan could not keep his eyes off Rosa when she walked by.

When Iris's friends were not with her, they discussed Rosa and Alan further. Their discussions revealed they were convinced that if the two were left in a room alone, Alan would definitely put his hands on Rosa, even make love to her. They did not dare go this far in their talks with Iris, though; because they had sworn they were her loyal friends. When they were with Iris and passed by Rosa at school or a social function outside school, they chided and snubbed Rosa. Iris's cronies did most of the chiding. Iris would carry herself publicly as if she were a shy person who would do harm to no one. And her apparent love of poetry—as evidenced by her carrying a book of poems with her at all times and excelling in class assignments pertaining to poetry—supported her genteel image. Still, Iris had a cold side. And that cold side caused Rosa to think Iris had never liked her.

Behind closed doors, Iris called Rosa terrible names and admitted she hated Rosa. "But Rosa will never have Alan," Iris declared to her friends. "He's pledged to me. His family and mine know we'll be married when Alan finishes law school, if not sooner. They've planned for us to marry each other ever since we were babies. We've always accepted that without question. Our parents know our union will make both families stronger. Of course our truly loving each other has never hurt that arrangement," she added with a coy smile.

Behind her back, Iris's friends pitied her for clinging to an arrangement that Iris's and Alan's parents made when the two were infants. They snickered at Alan for not being man enough to break off with Iris if he really wanted to play the field or if he just wanted someone else in particular. But then everyone in his and Iris's circle knew Alan was a mama's boy. Because he was an only child, his mother was easily able to focus her attention on steering Alan in the direction she wanted him to go.

Members of the Colored elite also knew that Alan's mother, the former Alice Newman, was money crazy; which was why she had married into the Covington family. She reared her son to have the values of the elite. Like his mother, Alan grew to love money, not only for the security it ensured but also for the status to which it elevated people like him and his family.

The Covingtons were well known for their wealth from real estate and other investments. Their family had used to their advantage what they had been bequeathed by their ancestors. During Reconstruction and beyond, their forefathers had become entrepreneurs and investors who steadily built upon their wealth and passed it on to their heirs.

Iris Haywood's parents owned homes on Martha's Vineyard, and also in Atlanta, and Philadelphia. Additionally they possessed money from Iris's grandparents' eateries in Atlanta and land holdings passed down through generations. Their land was inherited from slaves who had received it as gifts from benevolent slave masters.

*   *   *   *

The girls in Iris's circle whispered that if given a chance, they would go with Alan themselves. He was an easy-going guy with good looks and an excellent physique. What they did not seem to realize about Alan, however, was that he was very self-serving. He had indeed always acknowledged his and Iris's parents' arrangement for the two of them. That was expected. It was what one did when one was from a family like theirs. But knowing what he had going for himself physically, Alan seemed bound to take advantage of it and with whomever he chose.

Ever since Alan was about thirteen or fourteen years old, he had occasionally participated in boy-girl games that required the losers to disrobe in order to go to the next stage. Unbeknownst to Iris and other girls in and outside her circle, he had eventually had sex with many of their discreet but highly erotic friends. Alan was by outward appearances a conservative, shy but charming church boy. But behind closed doors he was so smooth and aggressive in his sexual explorations that he became an extremely desirable lover. Undercover, he had sex with every girl who would let him lift her skirt. Unlike many boys, he was not the kind that would have sex with a girl and tell. And that may have been why he won entry into more panties than most of his friends and associates did.

Alan eventually experienced Rosa sexually and discovered she was just as uninhibited and exploratory as he was. On top of that, she was both talented and intelligent. Soon he stopped trying to have sex with every girl in sight. He had sex with Iris to fulfill their families' pact. But he lay with Rosa every chance he got, as if he had been starving between their get-togethers. Rosa became his soul mate. No one else could satisfy him on all levels.

Even though they may have wanted to, Iris and her friends could not prevent Rosa from participating in the elite events in which they participated; because Rosa's mother and grandparents were just as educated and socially well connected as Iris's parents were. Occasionally, though, they did not have to worry about Rosa being around, like the time she became ill with a cold and fever and was forced to miss one of the most important events of the year.

CHAPTER 11

▼

"April in Paris," a scholarship fundraiser spearheaded by a group of Washington doctors' wives, was the event Rosa wanted so much to attend. It was going to be held at the Lincoln Colonnade, a dance hall behind the Lincoln Theater on U Street. D.C.'s elite and their teenage and young adult offspring were going to be there. Rosa knew that many of her popular schoolmates, including Alan Covington, were planning to attend.

However, Rosa's mother refused to let her attend the dance. Rosa insisted she felt better and cried prolifically in an effort to gain her way. Nevertheless, her mother did not soften on the issue. As a last ditch effort, Rosa slipped out of bed, bathed and dressed for the dance, and then insisted she was okay. But Nora still refused to let her go to the event.

In her persistence Rosa looked for her father and found him in the living room reading a newspaper. "Papa, may I please go to the April in Paris Dance over at the Lincoln Colonnade?"

"Go ask your mother, sweetheart," Douglas answered in a matter of fact tone, without looking up from the newspaper.

"Papa, do I have to? Can't you just let me go?"

This time he looked up from the paper. "No, I can't. Not without your mother's approval, too. Sorry, honey."

Her eyes brimming with tears, Rosa went back upstairs to her parents' bedroom, where her mother was still stretched out on the bed, engrossed in an art history book.

"Mama, please let me go to the dance," Rosa cried. "See, I'm all dressed," she said, pointing to her light green dress and jacket. She'd pulled most of her hair to the top of her head, and held it in place with hairpins and let the back hair hang loose below her neck and shoulders. Small golden earrings graced her ears and matching gold plated bracelets adorned her wrists. "Don't I look nice? I feel fine," she said, full of hope.

"I noticed your clothes, hairdo, and jewelry, when you came in here before. But while you may be dressed beautifully and think you feel fine, the truth is: your eyes look weak and watery. Your face looks like your resistance is low."

Rosa coughed involuntarily for several seconds, hating herself for not being able to control it. She looked down at her dressy black shoes a moment, then up at her mother.

"See?" Nora said. "You're still sick. You need to miss this dance and let yourself recuperate completely. You don't need to be going out into the night air. And you don't need to be sweating on some dance floor, and then coming back home sicker than you were before you left."

"Mama, please. Please. This is the most important dance of the year," Rosa pleaded, raising her voice.

Nora gave her a chastising look.

Rosa got the message. Her next plea was high pitched but low volume, almost the voice of a little girl. "Please let me go, Mama? Please, please?"

"No! Now don't ask me anymore," Nora shouted, her honey yellow-colored face flushed. She collected herself and in a gentler tone said, "Cool down, Rosa. Don't be so hot to trot. Your health is more important than any dance. I'm not letting you go out and catch even more cold, and then have to stay out of school next week."

Then, in a half playful and syrupy voice, Nora said, "Now go back to your room and take off those pretty clothes. Put your nightgown back on and get under the covers. I'll check on you later and bring you some soup and more cold medicine if you need it." Nora turned her eyes back to her book.

Rosa huffed and gave Nora a dreadful look. She knew she had exhausted her attempts at trying to sway her mother to let her go to the dance. She was miserable and viewed her mother's decision as dashing her opportunity to see Alan and be close to him.

Rosa hated being barred from the dance. The only way she could dissipate her anger and hurt was to call and talk to Elsie about it.

Elsie's parents were not letting her go to the dance either, Rosa learned. But Elsie sounded like it didn't matter to her as much as it did to Rosa. Elsie listened to Rosa vent for a while. Then she told Rosa a joke she had recently heard. They laughed together and moved on to other topics, like the Debutante Cotillion.

Seventeen year-old daughters of Washington's Colored elite were looking forward to the Cotillion with great anticipation.

CHAPTER 12

▼

Rosa really wanted to be a debutante in the cotillion sponsored by the Bachelor-Benedicts, the elite Colored men's social organization. In that annual event, about 20 young girls from some of Washington's oldest elite families were presented to society. Some of the girls participated in the cotillion only because their families expected it of them. Others participated with excitement, considering the event a milestone, a rite of passage in their lives.

Although Rosa desired to be a debutante, she didn't have an escort to the cotillion. She expressed her disappointment to Elsie. Elsie had no desire to be a part of the event, but listened to her best friend, as always, and tried to say things to make her feel better.

Rosa envied girls like Iris Haywood and others who knew well in advance who their escorts were going be. Everyone including Rosa knew that Iris's escort would be Alan Covington.

Rosa was crazy about Alan but temporarily let go of her dreams of having him. To solve her problem of securing a date for the cotillion, Rosa looked to one of her family members.

Grandpa William arranged for the grandson of one of his colleagues to escort Rosa to the Cotillion. Her escort, Thomas Wellington III, was reddish brown-skinned, tall, and good looking in a rugged sort of way. He attended all of the rehearsals for the cotillion with Rosa.

When the time came, Thomas donned a black tuxedo, white formal shirt, black bow tie, and black shoes. He escorted Rosa to the cotillion obviously with pride as she, dressed in a white organza gown, trimmed with white daisies, was presented to society along with all the other debutantes. It crossed her mind that this presentation to society might not be the real thing as far as Grandma Lilly was concerned, but it was certainly enough for Rosa. She enjoyed Thomas's company and remained grateful to him and Grandpa William for making it possible for her to attend the prestigious affair.

The following day, Rosa visited her best friend. She told Elsie all about the cotillion, perhaps the most significant event in Rosa's life before she rose to the next level: serious preparation for her career as a jazz singer. Elsie, who had not wanted to be a debutante and was not affected by the hoopla surrounding the event, nonetheless experienced it vicariously through Rosa.

With sparkling eyes and enthusiastic delivery, Rosa related every detail of the event to Elsie, including the fact that other debutantes had glared at her with envy and many escorts, including Alan Covington, had looked at her with desire in their eyes.

CHAPTER 13

▼

1944

After graduation, Rosa and her classmates went their own separate ways. Rosa entered Howard University as a Music Education major, at her mother's prodding, even though she preferred the prospect of performance art to the field of teaching. Nora argued that a major in Education would provide Rosa with a safety net in case, for whatever reason, her singing career was not fulfilled. Therefore Rosa majored in Education to satisfy her mother's reasoning and to keep her quiet regarding the one thing Rosa knew she was destined to do.

Rosa convinced herself that her grandmother had nothing to do with her decision to major in Music Education, and that she no longer cared what Grandma Lilly thought.

Elsie went to Miner Teachers College, declaring a major in Home Economics and a minor in Fashion Design.

Iris Haywood matriculated at Hampton Institute, in Virginia. Alan was headed back to Tennessee for his third year at Fisk. Many of the boys they all knew shipped out to serve in the war in Europe.

Rosa and Elsie were not interested in joining a sorority. However Rosa did pledge and was accepted into Delta Sigma Theta, in hopes of pleasing her mother. It was the Deltas who had awarded Nora the scholarship that assisted her in studying art at the prestigious Académie Julian in Paris, France, before Rosa was born.

The Alpha Kappa Alpha women were mostly light-skinned. Rosa knew of none who were as dark brown as she was. Her membership in the Deltas helped her lead a happier college life.

*   *   *   *

In her early college years at Howard University, Rosa held onto something special: her warm memories of stolen moments with Alan before he went to Fisk for his freshman year. It was during the summer following her sophomore year at Dunbar that he left town, headed for Fisk, in Memphis, Tennessee. Rosa was surprised early that Saturday morning when he stopped by her house. The doorbell rang. Other family members were upstairs or in the kitchen having breakfast. Still in her blue nightgown and pale pink terrycloth robe, she had been sitting in the living room perusing her sheet music.

When Rosa heard the sound of the doorbell, she opened the door and stepped onto the black-and-white tiled floor of the vestibule. She caught her breath before opening the second door that led to the porch. Through the lace-covered glass portion of the door, she saw Alan's pale light-skinned face. His close cut reddish brown hair looked shiny and healthy. He stood tall, his hands in his pockets, looking down at the cement porch. She pulled open the door. He looked up, saw her, and his face turned beet-red. She was elated but allowed only a slow smile to cross her face.

"Good morning," she said, not closing her robe.

"Hi," he said, smiling into her face, and then letting his eyes rove to her deep cleavage, which showed above the low-cut, lace trim bodice of her nightgown.

"You want to come in?" she asked, now smiling broadly.

"No, that's all right. I thought maybe we could take a walk…. and talk. I'm leaving for Fisk today, and I just wanted to say goodbye, or farewell, or whatever people say when they're going far away but know they'll be back at some point in time."

"Okay, I'll just be a minute," she told him. "I have to run upstairs and throw on a dress." Leaving the door ajar, she walked hurriedly back to the kitchen to let her mother know she was going to put on some clothes and go for a walk with Alan.

"All right," Nora said, smiling her approval. She had always seemed to like Alan.

After dressing and returning downstairs, Rosa glided to the front of the house and closed both doors behind her as she stepped out onto the porch, into the humid August air.

"You ready?" Alan said, his hands still in his pockets.

"Yes, I'm ready." Rosa smoothed her hair back on each side, letting it hang loosely, below her shoulders.

They walked up Summit Place to North Capitol Street and then turned right to round the corner. They sauntered past a few shops and grocery stores. Light automobile traffic and a few pedestrians passed them along their way.

"Rosa," Alan began, "I'll be gone for a long time. I might be back for Thanksgiving. If not, I know I'll be home for Christmas. I just want you to know I'll be thinking about you. You know I like you a lot, right?"

"Yes, I know. But you don't always act like it, especially when Iris and those other snobbish kids are around. You like Iris too, don't you? You've always liked her."

"Yeah, but it's not like it seems," he said, turning red. "See, her parents and my parents have always been good friends, since they were in college. When Iris and I were babies, our parents used to kid about arranging for us to get married one day. Then as the years passed, it seemed like they were really serious about it. By the time I was in junior high school, my mother started telling me that since both families were well off, and since Iris and I were both light-skinned and from the same background, we would make a good match. She said our children would be light-skinned too, and they would be highly intelligent and cultured because of their parents' and grandparents' bloodlines."

"That's crazy, and it's not fair. Not fair to you and not fair to me or any girl like me that you might end up liking better than Iris!" Rosa declared in an angry tone.

"I know it's not, but try telling my parents that and it's a losing battle," Alan said.

"Yeah, I guess you're right," she said.

"I know I'm right. Anyway, I just want you to know you're the girl I really like. Whenever I'm around you, I feel I love you. I mean I want you. But it's more than just physical. I like your personality, your ambition, your talent, everything about you. And it doesn't matter to me that you're dark-skinned. I love that about you. I'm always around too many people with no color and no spirit. They're just not down to earth like you are."

Rosa blushed openly and did not interrupt him.

"Ever since that time you kissed me in the hall at church during choir rehearsal, I've known you were the one. I just want you to know that before I hop on that train today."

"Thanks, Alan. I've always known how I feel about you. But I wasn't sure about your feelings, that's all."

"Now you know. I can't ask you to wait for me, but if you're still available when I finish law school, we could see where we stand then. It'll be my life, so if you and I want to be together after we finish our education, nobody can stop us."

"That's right," Rosa said with belief and determination in her voice.

They were nearing a tailoring shop that was next to a narrow clean alley and then a beauty shop. Neither establishment was open yet. Alan and Rosa walked into the empty alley and stood there for a while. He pulled her close, and then leaned down and planted his lips on her mouth. She parted her lips. He entered her mouth with his tongue, probing gently, deeply. She clung to him. For several minutes they held each other in a loving embrace, while enjoying their kiss. They became steamy, finding it hard to let go, until a group of elderly ladies with Bibles in their hands passed by the alley. The ladies were chatting and did not look Alan and Rosa's way, but their passing by alarmed the lovers enough to make them jump apart. For a few moments, they stood together without touching, and then Alan spoke.

"We'd better go," he said with reluctance. "But I'm glad we talked. I've got to go back home now. Gotta have breakfast with my parents. After breakfast, they're taking me to Union Station."

"I've got to go home for breakfast too," Rosa said. "But look, don't forget to write me, okay?" She felt in her heart she would always love him.

"I'll write you," he said. "I promise."

They held hands and started their walk back to Summit Place.

CHAPTER 14

▼

Washington, D.C.
1945

In April '45, about a month before the end of Rosa's first year at Howard University, U.S. President, Franklin Roosevelt, died. She was leaving the University Library when a few classmates rushed towards her with the news. She and her friends were stunned and stood huddled together in shock. They had never even thought about the possibility of a President dying while he was in office.

Rosa felt as if the whole country was in chaos and unprotected. After leaving her friends, she rushed home to talk about the astounding event with her family. Douglas and Nora comforted her and each other. Although surprised to hear the news, Willie and Dot did not have much to say. Neither of them appeared to grieve the Country's loss.

Grandma Lilly had little to say about Roosevelt's death, except "Maybe it's time for new blood in the White House anyway. After Harry Truman finishes out Roosevelt's term, maybe we can vote a Republican in there."

"To tell you the truth," she added, "I'm tired of having dull looking Eleanor Roosevelt as a First Lady. Well, we'll see what Vice President Truman will do, or should I say what *President* Truman will do for the country, now that they've sworn him in to take the helm."

William warned Lilly to stop talking negatively about Franklin and Eleanor Roosevelt. Although William was a Republican like Lilly, he respected Nora, Douglas, and Rosa's love of the deceased Democratic President and sympathized with them as they grieved over the loss of the country's long-time popular leader. "There are so many people in the country grieving right now, including Nora, Douglas, and Rosa. Let them grieve in peace, Lilly," William said.

His verbal reprimand made Lilly stop her negative talk about the late President and his widow, which meant Lilly had no more to say about them. She would respect William's words, because he so seldom opposed her on anything. When he did, she knew he meant business. Since he was the only one in their marriage who was working and bringing in money, Lilly did not seem to question his position as the leader in their relationship.

The War in Europe ended in September 1945. A bronze plaque of Franklin Roosevelt, by Selma Burke, a renowned Colored sculptor, was unveiled at the White House by President Harry S. Truman. Adding to that momentous event for Colored Americans that autumn, was John H. Johnson's publication of the first issue of Ebony Magazine.

*   *   *   *

Rosa was in her sophomore year at Howard University and missing Alan's presence in D.C. Alan, in his third year at Fisk, had been writing letters to Rosa; however, he gradually slowed to a halt. When he stopped writing her, she stopped writing him. She did not want to chase Alan. Chasing him would make her look pitiable, she thought. And, although generally she did not care what people thought, in this particular case she did care. Pitiable was the last image she wanted to project to Alan or anyone else.

Contrary to what Rosa anticipated, whenever Alan came home to Washington on holidays, he spent time with his family and with Iris. Rosa resented that. She figured he should at least steal away and come see her for a few hours during the holidays. Rosa concluded that either his mother insisted that he spend every moment with the family and Iris, or else Iris made a point of following him around every minute he was not with his family. In either case, though, what would have been wrong with him being man enough to pick up the telephone and call Rosa, or at least stop by Summit Place a minute and say hello to her? *Well...whatever,* she mused. She desperately wanted to see him, be with him and make love to him, but she refused to dwell on those feelings. Rosa's chief desire, the one she dreamed about all her life, took precedence over Alan. And she was going to fulfill that dream whether Alan, or any other boy for that matter, was in her life or not.

CHAPTER 15

▼

1947–1948

During her senior year at Howard, Rosa performed a semester of practice teaching at Dunbar High School. She taught theory plus music appreciation classes and covered classical, sacred, and popular music with her students. But she found that many of her students adored the new style of jazz music called Bebop, a fast-paced, intricate style forged by alto saxophonist Charlie Parker and trumpet player, Dizzy Gillespie. Both musicians played solo in small clubs in New York and elsewhere, and performed in jam sessions after hours. They were helping to launch a musical revolution. Unlike Swing, their style of music was for listening rather than dancing. People seemed to either embrace the new style or hate it. Many of Rosa's students loved it. After she finished her lesson plan each class session, she allowed time for the students to talk informally about the new music craze.

Students talked about the new ways of drumming introduced by Bebop, in which musicians like Kenny Clarke and other drummers interacted with the horns. Rosa's classes also discussed jazz piano players they were hearing about, such as Theolonius Monk, who, like other bebop musicians in New York, played at Minton's, the famed club on 52nd Street between 5th and 6$^{th.}$ That location—a single block of old brownstones on the west side of New York City—was called "The Street," Rosa told her students. It became known as Harlem Downtown.

Other students of Rosa's continued their loyalty to the big bands and their leaders, like Duke Ellington and Count Basie. They had a special affection for Duke Ellington, since he was originally from Washington, D.C.

The principal of Dunbar and Rosa's classical-minded colleagues didn't like the idea of Rosa allowing discussions about Jazz to go on in her classroom, even if the discussions were happening after she had finished her lesson plans based on the required curriculum. But Rosa paid them no attention. She knew she was not going to be teaching school for very long, so she refused to let their disapproval bother her.

In addition to teaching Music Appreciation and Theory, Rosa worked with students who were in rehearsals for a musical play. Some of the budding musical theater actors were also in Rosa's other music classes. They responded to her earthy personality and broad outlook on life.

Rosa's friend Elsie moved in a different direction. Elsie had dropped out of Miner Teachers College in her third year, along with her classmate and boyfriend, Jimmy Webb. Elsie was pregnant, so she and Jimmy got married. They were expecting a baby later that year, and wanted to get a start making money to support themselves and the baby after it was born.

While she was pregnant, Elsie employed her sewing skills by working for a tailoring shop. She took in work as a freelance seamstress on the side. Elsie also designed hats for affluent Colored ladies in D.C. She had been inspired to pursue hat designing since high school, after she saw a hat created by Colored New York designer Mildred Blount featured on the cover of *Ladies' Home Journal*.

Jimmy, who was a tall, hefty but graceful young man, took the test to enter employment with the Federal Government. He passed the test and secured a job in the mailroom at the Navy Department.

Elsie still kept in touch with Rosa but not as much as she had in high school and during their early college years. Elsie and Jimmy spent most of their time working, and when they were not working, they were together enjoying each other and making plans for the future. They were living in Jimmy's parents' home and preparing one of the rooms there for use as a nursery, Elsie told Rosa during a phone talk that spring. She also told Rosa they planned to stay with Jimmy's parents for a few years, until they were able to afford a place of their own. And she said eventually she and Jimmy wanted to be totally on their own.

Rosa missed talking to Elsie almost every day and desperately missed their previous close friendship. But she was forced to understand that they had less in common now. Elsie had to devote most of her attention to her husband and later that year to the new baby as well, if she wanted her marriage and family life to succeed. Realizing that Elsie had to focus on her nuclear family, Rosa started contacting a few of her single sorority sisters more often and socializing with them. However, she knew she'd always regard Elsie as her best friend.

Rosa was looking forward to graduating from Howard University and to spending the summer visiting some D.C. nightspots. She intended to meet a number of club managers in her preparation for her move into the professional world.

At the time, Jazz Vocalist Sarah Vaughan was extremely popular, having already topped the charts with the song, "Tenderly", and having won a Top Female Vocalist Award by the Down Beat and Metronome jazz magazines. Rosa admired Sarah Vaughan, who was only a few years older than she was. However, Rosa was careful to polish her own vocal techniques, so that her style wouldn't be unduly influenced by Sarah Vaughan's. Rosa was striving to be unique.

Having been offered a fulltime teaching position in the school system, Rosa planned to teach voice and piano classes in the fall, while continuing to test the waters as a part-time professional performer at the Lincoln Theater and certain D.C. nightclubs. She was not going to plan her move to New York right away. She would first try to convince her parents, especially her mother, to see her view of her goal. She knew her father would approve and wish her well. But it was important to Rosa to secure moral support from both her parents, even though, now that she was grown and self-supporting, she could do what she wanted to do.

Rosa knew Grandma Lilly would remain true to form and disapprove of her goals. But Rosa nearly convinced herself she no longer cared what her grandmother thought. Grandma Lilly had always made remarks to threaten Rosa's self-esteem and to influence her to let go of her dreams. She had never treated Rosa to the degree of attention and affection that she had showered on Dot. Well, Rosa declared to herself, *I am not a child anymore, and I don't need Grandma Lilly's approval on anything!*

CHAPTER 16

▼

Washington, D.C.
1949

During her second year as a teacher at Dunbar, Rosa celebrated her twenty-second birthday. Later that year, in October, she had a reunion with an important person from her past. When she met with him this time, he'd earned the title, Attorney at Law. Alan had finished Harvard Law School, then worked for a while at a Colored law firm in Philadelphia and served on the Human Rights commission there. Now he was back in his hometown to start work at Walker, Thomas, and Scott, a prominent Colored law firm. He was also planning to be married.

Because Alan was soon to marry Iris Haywood, some of the women he knew would have been afraid or at least hesitant to have an affair with him, but not Rosa. Her in-college socializing with fast girl friends and her sexual, as well as platonic, experiences with worldly boys had added to her natural fearlessness where people were concerned. She had started going with friends to dance halls like the Lincoln Colonnade on 12th and U streets, as well as the Odd Fellows Hall on 9th and T. She and her friends frequented popular spots like Brown's Lodge, a club on "U" Street between 13th and 14th—and clubs where vocalists such as Ella Fitzgerald, Billie Holiday, Nat King Cole, and Pearl Bailey performed, when they were in town. Rosa paid to see these artists and others, like Lena Horne and Sammy Davis Jr., when they appeared at the Howard Theater.

Rosa and the friends she selected sometimes dressed up and visited Thurston's Grille on 9th near "U" Street. A very classy establishment, Thurston's had just one vocalist performing. Rosa began to frequent Thurston's and other clubs more. That frequency made her more worldly and excited about late nightlife. At night she was a flower in bloom.

One night Rosa connected with Alan instead of joining friends at a club, as she had promised she would do. Alan picked her up at home, after leaving the law firm where he worked. When he showed up at her door, he was in a tan trench coat, unbuttoned and revealing his brown pinstriped suit with wide lapels, the cream-colored dress shirt, and a brown and tan print tie. He had on dark brown shoes. His red hair was short and neat. He smiled, and his face flushed with excitement, when Rosa answered the doorbell.

"Well, hello," she greeted him, her stomach aflutter, as she let a slow smile brighten her face.

"Hi, baby. You look gorgeous," he said, letting his smile have free reign. He surveyed her from head to toe, taking in her upswept curls, small dangling gold earrings, and her form-fitting dark green dress with white polka dots. On the front of her dress she had fastened a piece of jewelry, a red rose, which Elsie had given her for her birthday.

"I like that dress," Alvin said.

"Thank you." Her smile was full. "Hang on for a minute. I'll just grab my jacket and be right out."

While waiting for her on the small square porch, he did a slow 360 degree turn and looked down at the grassy plots on either side of the cement landing, and then down the second set of steps to the sidewalk.

He could hear her grandmother's scolding remark. "You know you have no business going out with another woman's fiancé!" Lilly shouted.

Rosa ignored her grandmother.

"Did you hear what I said young lady?" Lilly continued to shout. "Your mother and father won't like what you're doing either, when I tell them. What you're doing is not right. Do you hear me?"

Pursing her lips, Rosa said coldly, "Yes, Grand*mother*," she answered in a sarcastic tone. "I *hear* you." She added nothing to soften her curt reply, but simply closed the door behind herself and joined Alvin. "Let's go," she said.

Together they descended the steps to the sidewalk, where Alvin's black sedan was parked. He never drove his two-seated maroon sports car when he was going on a tryst with Rosa. She liked his sports car, but she knew why he used the black sedan when he was with her. It wouldn't draw undue attention to them.

He opened the passenger door for her, then strode around to the driver's side, and slid under the wheel. Soon they were headed down the street.

He drove to a small Colored-owned hotel in Northeast D.C., where no one knew him or his family or social circle. It was the place he and Rosa used to go to when they wanted to be together in private and make love. Sometimes they would go to dinner first, at a place near 8th and H Streets, Northeast, that Rosa liked and where, again they were not likely to run into anyone who knew Alvin, his family, or friends. They would eat a hearty dinner, listen to the band or jukebox play, and enjoy each other's company in a public place before continuing their evening privately in the hotel. Alvin had checked in and paid for the room beforehand and under a different name. He had then left and picked up Rosa.

This evening, when they arrived at the restaurant, no band was in the house. After he and Rosa selected a table, he went across the room to the jukebox, dropped money in it and pushed a few buttons. As his first selection, George Gershwin's *Our Love Is Here To Stay*, started playing, he headed back to the table and joined Rosa.

"You knew I'd like that one, huh?" she asked.

"Yes, I knew," Alan responded.

She smiled into his eyes and placed her hand on his thigh under the table. The waiter took their order and disappeared.

Rosa and Alvin talked about their jobs and their dreams for the future. They chatted about their families, laughing at incidents they considered amusing. Neither of them mentioned Iris.

CHAPTER 17

▼

October 1949

On a sunny, color-splashed day in October, Rosa auditioned at Brown's Lodge. Tommy Brown hired her on the spot, complimenting her on her unique vocal style and rich voice. He could not give her solo billing at the time, he said, but he would let her work as a warm up act for the veteran performer who already had a contract there. He promised Rosa that when that contract ended, he would offer her solo billing if she still wanted it.

One Friday night at Brown's, Rosa appeared in an off-white dress and heels, wearing her curled hair upswept and held in place with hairpins and a silk open red rose above one ear. The number she opened with was *I Get a Kick Out of You.* When she ended the song, she smiled in response to the applause from the audience and thanked them with a slight bow. She raised her head as the band played a few bars of *It Had to Be You*, and she knew it was time for her to sing again. Rosa followed that ballad with one other tune.

After singing *They Can't Take That Away From Me*, Rosa left the stage and sat at a large round table with Elsie and her husband, Jimmy, a couple of her colleagues from Dunbar High School and their husbands. One of Rosa's sorority sisters and her boy friend also sat at the table with them. While enjoying their compliments and conversation, Rosa glanced around the room, and she spotted her brother Willie. He was sitting and drinking with a group who appeared to be older than his seventeen years.

Rosa knew Willie was allowed into the club only because he looked twenty-one with his height, weight, and the thin mustache he had cultivated. Willie and a few of the young men he sat with wore suits. Willie had on a dark blue one, while a few of his friends wore tan, or dark gray suits with light shirts and dark ties, and others were dressed in slacks and sweaters or slacks and casual shirts and jackets. The women in Willie's group had on dressy black outfits, or colorful solid or print dresses or blouses and skirts. Willie and his friends' and girlfriends' outfits were typical of all the club's customers. All wore happy faces as they chatted and laughed at each other's stories and jokes. They were obviously enjoying themselves sitting around large tables in the spacious room. At the front of the room, dark-suited musicians on stage played swing music. Cigarette smoke floated around the room, mingling with the odor of clashing colognes, body musk, and hard liquor.

At Willie's table was a strikingly beautiful woman seated next to and leaning into him. She looked much older than Willie. The mystery woman was at least thirty, Rosa thought. Choosing not to embarrass Willie, however, Rosa did not go to his table.

*   *   *   *

Later Willie's friends, having pulled on their jackets and coats, were ready to leave the club before Rosa's group was. Some people in Willie's party glanced in the direction of Rosa's table as they headed towards the exit. It was then that Rosa was sure the thirty-something woman was Willie's date. Her slender, brown coated figure leaned into him as they walked, and she helped steady him as they neared the exit. Her light skin had a pinkish tone with a hint of olive. And her straight light brown hair, turned under at the ends, fell to her shoulders.

If the woman had consumed a lot of liquor, it did not show. She held Willie up as he staggered, suit jacket open, shirt hanging outside his pants and his tie loosened, slurring his words while passing by Rosa's table.

Rosa knew Willie did not see her when he and his mysterious woman passed by. She fought hard her impulse to rise from her table and ask him what was going on. Not wanting to create a scene, she thought it would be better to pull him aside at home and give him a dose of her opinion about his behavior.

CHAPTER 18

▼

Willie was slurping orange juice when Rosa joined him in the kitchen the next day, around one o'clock. As she entered the room, he looked up. "Well, good morning, songbird, the next Ella Fitzgerald."

"No, silly. I admire Ella. She's really talented. But just call me by my own name: Rosa Johnson Stills, jazz singer," Rosa said, waiving one hand flamboyantly and pulling a cup from a cabinet with the other.

"You're definitely on your way," he said, and then gulped down more juice and set his cup on the table. "I stopped by Brown's Lodge last night with some friends. We saw you singing before the regular act came on. You were good. The crowd loved you!"

Rosa smiled. "What can I say? It's what I was born to do," she said in a matter of fact tone. She then pulled the pot of freshly made coffee from the stove top and poured some into her cup. "Did you make this coffee?" she asked.

"No, I think either Mama or Grandma made it," Willie replied.

"By the way," Rosa asked, "Who was that woman you were with?

"What woman?" Willie asked.

"I'm talking about the tall, light-skinned woman. The one with brown hair," Rosa said between sips of coffee.

While Rosa waited for Willie's answer, Dot strolled into the kitchen, modeling an off-white satin robe and matching slippers. She ran her hand along the side of her tousled sandy-colored hair in a smoothing gesture. The hair immediately flopped back to its disheveled state. "He probably doesn't know which one," she blurted in Rosa's direction.

At age fifteen, Dot was described by her friends as gorgeous. She was tall and slender, with creamy light skin, and fine naturally curly hair that hung well below her shoulders. However, her personality was attractive only to her grandmother Lilly and to her friends. Dot had developed into a conceited and snooty ingénue. Of Nora and Douglas's three children, she was the only one who always addressed their grandmother as Grand*mother* Lilly. Rosa and Willie persisted in calling her Grand*ma* Lilly; which never earned them any points with Lilly through the years. But as Dot became the kind of adolescent that assured she would become a young woman who would, according to her grandmother, *succeed in society*, Lilly bragged about her and continued to show that Dot was her favorite grandchild.

"Why do you say that, Dot," Willie asked. "Not that anybody asked you to butt into our conversation. But since you're in it, why do you say that?"

"Because you have so many girlfriends you can't keep track of them.

And between the girlfriends and the liquor, it's a wonder if you really know who you are!" Dot said, opening the refrigerator and pulling out the milk. She then pulled a box of sweet buns from one cabinet above the counter and a glass from the other.

Willie looked at Rosa. "Don't pay any attention to Dot. She's just a freshman and doesn't know what's going on in school or anywhere else, let alone what I'm doing."

Pouring milk in her glass, Dot said, "Willie, you don't know what you're talking about. I'm the most popular girl in my class and I know more than you think I know."

"What you really are is a spoiled brat ruined by Grandma and idolized by your little friends who think they're God's gift to the world," Willie said. "And whatever you know, it's not relevant here, so butt out."

"Hmpf!" Dot uttered, before biting into a sweet bun.

Willie then returned his attention to Rosa. "So who're you talking about?"

"What do you mean, who? You know who I mean. That older woman holding you up when you looked like you were falling down drunk. The one who left the club with you and who probably brought you home too, judging by your condition last night."

Willie looked pensive for a moment. "Oh, yeah. You must mean Goldie."

"Goldie! Goldie who?" Rosa demanded. She had already figured out who Goldie was, but she wanted to see if Willie knew or would tell the truth about her.

Dot was sitting at the kitchen table, eating her bun, sipping her milk, and appeared to be amused at her siblings' conversation.

"Goldie Taylor," Willie replied. "You know her don't you?" he asked Rosa. Goldie graduated from Howard. She's an AKA," he added.

"Even I know who she is," Dot injected, between chews. "Her baby sister is in one of my classes."

"Nobody asked you, Dot," Rosa said. You know you can dismiss yourself whenever you want. This is a private conversation, okay?"

Dot rose from the table. "Well, never let it be said I stay where I'm not wanted. There are too many people who do want me. As a matter of fact I'm going to get dressed right now and join some of them at a friend's house," she said as she left the kitchen without removing her empty milk glass and pastry crumbs from the table.

"Have fun," Rosa said with sarcasm in her voice.

Rosa then said to Willie, "So Goldie must've come out of Howard ten years ago. She's obviously much older than we are."

"Well, yeah. She's older. But she looks young doesn't she? She looks real good, too," he added, his eyes lighting up.

"Oh, she looks good all right. But I don't think you should be messing with her. Don't you think she's way out of your league?"

"Why do you say that?" Willie asked, not looking at Rosa.

"After your group left the club, I thought about where I'd seen her. She used to be married to Paul Nelson. I don't know if they're divorced, but even when she was with him, she was sleeping around with other men, and she was known to be a heavy drinker."

"Yeah. But Rosa, she can hold her liquor. That woman knows she can party and hold her liquor at the same time!"

"Yeah," Rosa said curtly. "And I guess she can do a certain other thing really good too, since you're hanging around her like she's your girlfriend."

"She is, kind of. But not my main girl." Then he frowned. "But that's really my business. I'm a man. I know how to handle myself," he said.

"Yeah, well just be careful. You don't want to disgrace yourself with Mama and Papa. And you *know* you don't want to disgrace Grandma Lilly. She'd go crazy over any scandal involving you or Dot. Now if something exploded with me, she'd just say she expected it, but with her pets it would be a different story."

"I'm not Grandma Lilly's pet. It's Dot all the way, as far as Grandma's concerned."

"That might be true. But she favors you more than she does me. I can tell by her actions and her words. You know yourself, she's color struck."

Willie grabbed a roll from a saucer on the table, bit into it, and between chews mumbled, "That's true. She can't help it I guess. That's how she was brought up. It's how a lot of people are these days too." He looked pensive a moment and then said, "As long as Mama and Papa don't discriminate, that's all I care about. They're the ones who really love us and do things for us. Grandpa William is all right too, you know?"

"Yeah, he is. Anyway, back to what we were talking about. Are you going to straighten up and carry yourself the way you should, or not. I don't think you should take this lightly, Willie."

"Okay, okay, I get the point, Rosa. Just drop it, all right?"

"Sure, but remember: It's not always what you do, but how you do it. So if you're going to be out there acting wild and drinking a lot, don't come home. Have one of your buddies call and tell Mama you're going to stay at a friend's house overnight. That way you can sober up before you come home."

"All right! Now would you please let me finish eating my breakfast in peace?" He said curtly, his slight hangover darkening his normally jovial disposition.

"Okay, baby brother," Rosa said, as she tilted the spout of the coffee pot over the rim of her cup and poured just enough into the cup to warm up the brew that turned lukewarm during their conversation. She knew Willie heard her advice but was not sure he would follow it.

CHAPTER 19

▼

1949

The next week, Alan telephoned Rosa. During the conversation they agreed to meet at their usual rendezvous. Rosa had no qualms about having an affair with a man who was going to marry someone else. She reasoned: He's not married *yet*.

Dressed in evening attire, they met at Thurston's Grille and enjoyed a meal with a bottle of wine, while listening to a local singer do a couple of sets. Rosa shared with Alan her dream of working in New York. Alan was infected with her excitement.

He offered to drive her to New York the next weekend. They could reserve a hotel room, Alan said, and survey the New York nightclub scene. Rosa could then talk to a few club owners. They could spend two nights in a hotel and return to D.C. on Sunday.

*   *   *   *

Putting Alan's suggestions to work in New York the following weekend, Rosa talked with several club owners and performed auditions for them. During each session, her confidence shone and her talent proved magnanimous. Rosa's beauty and shapely fullness were impossible to ignore. The club owners' immediate interest in her as a total package let Rosa know she could indeed secure a gig in the City.

Rosa was ecstatic over her successful auditions. Having Alan there to share that success with her made it even better. She had waited for this moment of proof all her life. She knew that once she started working in New York, jazz singing would be the only work she would ever do.

On their way back to the hotel, Alan bought a bottle of champagne. In their room, they drank a toast, and slowly downed the remainder of the libation while recapping the positive, negative, and humorous words and behaviors of the club owners for whom Rosa had auditioned.

Feeling mellow, Rosa kissed Alan. They began unfastening each other's clothes. He unbuttoned the front of her dress. She unbuttoned his shirt, and then unzipped his pants. He pulled down her skirt. They tugged at each other's underwear. Rosa pulled down his briefs and wriggled out of her panties. He unhooked her bra and slipped it off of her. Both naked, they wet kissed and slow danced their way into the bedroom and lowered themselves onto the bed. Each wanting control, they struggled a minute over who would be on top. Rosa won. She straddled him and kissed her way down his face to his neck. After circling his ear with her tongue, she darted in and out, breathing streams of warm breath into his ear. She kissed and licked her way down his chest to his stomach and then owned his manhood. He ran his hands through her hair as she gave him more pleasure than any woman he'd ever been with. Knowing he would explode any minute, she said, "Not yet, not yet." She mounted him and then rocked and rolled until he could hold it no longer, until she was on the verge of ecstasy. Together they reached the mountaintop, peaking, shouting each other's names. She arched her torso backwards, and then slumped forward on top of him. Released, the lovers fell asleep with Rosa on top. They lay that way until morning.

C H A P T E R 20

▼

1949

After returning to D.C., Rosa and Alan realized they could not stay away from each other for long periods of time. They met each week for about a month, continuing to enjoy their torrid love affair. Rosa finally asked Alan to break his engagement to Iris.

"You know I can't do that, Rosa," he said. "But I'll always make a way to be with you, even after Iris and I are married."

"I don't want to share you, Alan. Why don't you just break off with Iris. You know you don't love her," Rosa said, trying to remain calm.

"I can't quit her. It wouldn't be right. My family and her family are long-time friends. I told you before. When we were babies, our parents made a pact to make sure Iris and I would marry when we came of age. They wanted that for us so we could add to the money in both families, and so our children could carry on our line of wealth, light skin, and high intellect. That's not important to me, because I love people for who they are, not for what color they are or how much money they make. But my parents are different. And I was raised to respect them and their wishes.

"My mother has reminded me of the pact time and time again. Iris and I have gone together since junior high school—elementary school, really. Now we're engaged, so everybody expects the marriage to happen. It's the right thing for me to do—to follow through with it, I mean. But, Rosa, you've got to understand that my relationship with you will never suffer."

"Yeah, I've heard that story about your family's precious arrangement with Iris's family. And it has nothing to do with me. I mean I don't have to respect it."

"Well I do, Rosa."

"No you don't. Not if you're a real man."

"You never questioned my manhood before," Alan said, his face beet red.

"Well I am now. I think you're a mama's boy. You're weak if you can't run your own life now that you're grown."

"I guess I really can't expect you to understand, Rosa. All I can say is that the arrangement between my family and Iris's is something I have to abide by. I'm not going to argue with you about it anymore."

Realizing she would not win an argument with him over that issue, and that it was the only matter in which she could not be dominant in their relationship, Rosa decided to drop the subject.

She began consoling herself with the thought that living in New York might help her get over the fact that Alan was going to marry Iris. Nothing would change between Alan and herself. She knew he really belonged to her. *But who knows?* She thought. *Maybe one day I'll grow tired of sharing him. I might stop settling for being his mistress, the woman who has to stay under cover, remain discreet.*

Rosa began trying to convince herself that living and working in New York might help her get over Alan. The new level in her career, plus life in a new city might cause her to forget his touch completely. She would be meeting new people. Maybe she would fall in love with someone new, she reasoned.

CHAPTER 21

▼

Willie followed through on his promise to be discreet; however, he kept drinking heavily. Word traveled back to Rosa that her brother was a lush. Rosa warned Willie that he would become an alcoholic if he did not cut back drastically. Willie insisted he was just a social drinker and had everything under control.

Against her better judgment, Rosa accepted Willie's defensive answer and stopped criticizing him. But she knew Willie's close friends were beyond the point of being social drinkers. Some of them could not control their drinking. In her heart she knew Willie could not. But since he insisted on remaining in denial, there was nothing she could do to make him reduce or stop his drinking.

Willie was old enough to take responsibility for his own actions, Rosa reasoned; so she was going to let him go, emotionally. She did not intend to let Willie and his lifestyle infringe upon her plans and dreams.

Sure she loved Willie. Rosa loved her whole family, but she was determined not to let caring about their welfare drive her off track. She would always make herself available to them in an emergency situation, but she was determined to remain focused on her own life and career.

*   *   *   *

That autumn, Willie's drinking became worse. He did not socialize without drinking alcohol. One night he stumbled home drunk. He raised such a raucous that he woke up everyone in the house. As far as his parents and grandparents knew, that was the first time Willie had done such a thing. They brushed it off as a "boys will be boys" episode. After determining he was safe, they simply told him to go to bed.

When they woke up the next morning, Nora and Douglas decided Willie might need a talking to after all. Nora ate breakfast in the dining room with her parents; so that Douglas could sit in the kitchen with Willie and talk to him semi-privately. Douglas spoke to Willie about where heavy drinking could lead and emphasized how it could ruin any career Willie might plan. He got Willie to promise not to drink as a habit when he was with his friends. Willie gave his word but broke his promise the very next time he was with his buddies. And he kept on breaking it. He just kept it away from his family.

*   *   *   *

Willie managed to get into Howard University, but he partied so much that he did not study enough. His friends did his assignments for him and helped him cheat to pass his exams.

Willie barely graduated with a degree in liberal arts. As he had been strong in only one subject, English, he secured a job at the local Colored newspaper, which did not pay much. He wrote articles for the paper during the day and partied at night. Constant partying made him late for work, forget interviews he had scheduled, and miss deadlines he was working against. The publisher did not want to fire Willie, because he knew Willie's parents and grandparents. But eventually, the publisher pressured Willie to quit, telling him that if he left on his own, the newspaper would not have to tell his family about his poor job performance. Furthermore, the publisher told Willie, the newspaper would provide him with a good letter of reference should he need one while trying to secure another job.

Willie decided to resign. After leaving the newspaper, he elicited the help of his girlfriend.

Emma worked for the Federal Government and knew the right way to complete the government's application and take the test. With Emma's help, Willie obtained a job in the Navy Department, as a clerk. Soon afterwards, out of overwhelming gratitude, Willie proposed to Emma. He was not sure if he loved her, he told Rosa. But he genuinely liked Emma. She was fairly good looking: medium height and weight, with pecan brown skin and a quiet but pleasant personality. Additionally Emma had a good sense of humor and a good head on her shoulders, Willie added to Rosa, convincing her of Emma's worthiness to be his fiancée.

Willie began staying with Emma in her pre-furnished apartment on Gates Street more than he stayed at home. Her apartment was a couple of miles north of Summit Place. Since he had a Federal Government Job, he felt secure enough to help Emma pay the rent. They were the picture of a domesticated couple for a short while. Then they started going to parties given by free spirited single and married couples they knew. As a result, Willie began to drink even heavier than he did during his college days. Emma, who was a light drinker and knew her limit, detested the way Willie behaved when he was drunk. He was verbally abusive towards her and sloppy, leaving his soiled clothing and dirty dishes strewn over the apartment. He would go to work every day but stop off at a club or a buddy's house and drink before returning home. He also neglected his promise to Emma and his dad that he would try to stop drinking. They urged him to get professional help but he refused, saying he could handle his liquor and he could stop anytime he wanted to stop.

He was challenged to keep Emma from finding liquor bottles he had hidden in kitchen cabinets, under the sink, under the bed, in closets behind luggage and other items. Willie's verbal abuse of Emma, plus his evident preference for drinking over his desire to please her caused Emma to reach her limit. She told him she wanted him to move out. He staunchly refused to be put out.

A few mornings later, Emma did not get out of bed as usual to prepare to go to work. She told Willie she had a terrible headache and was not going to work that day. When Willie left the apartment, saying he was on his way to work, Emma waited long enough to be sure he was gone for sure. Then she slipped out of bed, took her engagement ring off her finger and placed it on the dresser. A couple of friends Emma telephoned agreed to help her move her clothes and personal effects out of the apartment and into her best girlfriend's place.

By the time Willie returned from work that evening, Emma was gone. He found her ring on the dresser. Next to the ring was a note telling Willie she was gone for good and that he should not try to locate her or contact her.

Without Emma's support, Willie fell behind on the rent and lost the apartment. With his reputation for being an alcoholic, none of his friends or associates would allow him to live with them. Therefore, he had to move back into his family's home.

Nora and Douglas did not like what their son had become, but Nora was tolerant and tried to help him find a job. Douglas was not so tolerant. He stayed on Willie's case, lecturing him about the responsibilities involved in marriage. Even if he and Emma never got back together, Willie still needed to grow up and face the truth, Douglas told him. He needed to be a responsible human being. He needed to work. After all, Douglas told him, "If working steady is good enough for your father and both of your grandfathers, then working steady should be good enough for you."

While Nora was often in denial of Willie's alcoholism, Douglas nagged him about joining a support group for alcoholics.

Nevertheless, Willie sponged off of Nora and Douglas. His grandfather William never judged him and was always willing to talk with him without lecturing him. Dot, at nineteen years old, was not judgmental of Willie at all. Having a large circle of friends plus a boyfriend who was a law professor at Howard, Dot was immersed in her own life. Therefore she spoke with Willie in a civil, often light-hearted manner, telling him amusing stories about her friends and college life.

Willie could not tolerate his father's constant display of disapproval, like Douglas's behavior on the night that proved to be the culmination of a string of heated arguments they had been having.

"Willie, you're my only son," Douglas said. "I want you to make something of yourself. Not necessarily in a highbrow way like becoming a lawyer or doctor or something your grandmother would want you to be. I want you to go into whatever field you want to go into, do whatever job you want to do. I just want you to be responsible...respectable...have some self-control. Don't let anything like alcohol or drugs control you and mess up your life."

"Papa, you're taking this thing way out of proportion. Sure I drink a little around the house. And I drink when I go out with my friends. Its just being sociable, that's all. It's nothing that's going to keep me from having a good job or a career."

"Willie, I've said this to you before, and I'll say it again: Drinking every day is not sociable or recreational drinking. Drinking every day is a habit. You're an alcoholic. Now I want you to admit it. I want you to get some help, some treatment."

"I don't know where you're getting your information from, Papa, but I am not an alcoholic," Willie insisted in a raised voice. I can stop whenever I want. I just happen to like drinking when I want to drink, that's all," he added loudly.

"The thing most alcoholics have in common is that they're in denial. I want you to see Dr. Peterson and let him help you or refer you to a specialist," Douglas said firmly. "Then you join a support group, or you will *not* keep living here. That's final!"

Appearing exasperated, Willie didn't say another word. He strode out of the living room, climbed the stairs and went to his bedroom. He grabbed a suitcase, stuffed it with clothing and personal items, walked purposefully down the stairs, and dashed out of the house, slamming the front door behind him.

CHAPTER 22

▼

1949

Rosa re-connected with Alan at a party she attended with friends. Proceeds collected were slated for an AKA Sorority sponsored scholarship fund. Seeing Alan again was wonderfully disturbing for Rosa. The two spotted each other simultaneously. The chemistry was instant. Alan wore a charcoal-colored suit with an off-white shirt and print tie.

Their eyes locked. Alan looked Rosa up and down, smiling his approval of her curly hairdo and the low cut red dress she had on. Rosa felt as if he could see through her clothes, to her naked body, as his eyes appraised her from head to toe. Iris was with him.

Iris's light skin used to look pale during the years her hair was a dull red. But she had finally bloomed and become an attractive, flaming red-head. Although she was a member of the Alpha Kappa Alpha Sorority, Iris was still quiet. At least in public she was quiet. She was the picture of shyness and gentility. But behind closed doors she was more vocal and spoke her true mind about matters that disturbed her or people she disliked.

Covey, as Alan's friends began calling him, had with his aristocratic carriage a reserved demeanor but a warm smile that lit up his face. His smile, good looks, and conservative manner always captivated Rosa, just as her bold ways, pretty features, mocha-hued skin and voluptuous figure always ignited his desire.

Before the event was over, Rosa and Alan slipped away from the party room and found their way to the front porch, where they chatted and flirted heavily with each other. Alan then latched onto Rosa's arms and closed the space between them. She melted into his body immediately and held up her mouth to him. He pressed his lips against hers; entering her mouth and probing deeply with his warm tongue. Surrendering to his kiss, she pressed her body closer to his.

He gripped her below the waist, and then slipped his hands to the sides of her hips and buttocks, pressing her into him, claiming her. Just as urgently, he released her and stared into her eyes with longing.

"When can we—

—"Oh, *here* you are, Alan," Iris said, without acknowledging Rosa. Her slender figure moved gracefully in the lavender dress and matching shoes she wore. Her upswept red hair, light makeup, and pink lipstick gave her a sophisticated image. "I was looking for you."

Annoyed at being interrupted, Rosa gave Iris a sharp look.

Alan was red-faced and embarrassed.

Iris continued, as if nothing was amiss. "There are people inside who want to meet you, sweetheart. Let's not keep them waiting," she said, taking Alan's hand and leading him toward the door to the house. She ignored Rosa.

"*Hello*, Iris," Rosa said, in a commanding tone, forcing Iris to acknowledge her presence.

"Oh. Hi," Iris answered in a clipped cadence, without slowing her gait or looking at Rosa, or even saying Rosa's name.

At the door leading into the house, Alan let go of Iris's hand.

Iris looked at Alan. "Well—are you going back in with me or not?" she snapped.

"All right, Iris," Alan replied in an unwilling yet docile tone.

Iris glared back at Rosa, then turned and strode into the house with Alan following her. He stepped inside the house, without looking back at Rosa.

Rosa lingered on the porch alone for a few minutes, before walking quietly back inside the house. She made her excuses to the hostess and to the young women with whom she had arrived there. Rosa then left the party.

Briskly she walked several blocks back to her family's home, thinking along the way of nothing but her tryst with Alan. Now that they had reconnected and in such a passionate manner, she knew they were truly meant to be. Fate had thrown them back into each other's arms, and there was no way she was going to let him out of her life again. Even though she was planning to go to New York to begin living her professional dream, she would also be thinking of ways she and Alan could be together.

Alan's and Iris's parents' may have vowed long ago to make them marry each other, but it was really *she* and Alan who were meant to be. Alan's and Iris's parents and Iris just kept getting in the way. *Let them*, Rosa thought. *I don't care what any of them do. Alan Covington is mine and I don't care what I have to do to keep him!*

CHAPTER 23

▼

November 1949

Rosa's thoughts about her life up to the day of her grandmother's death finally made her fall asleep. Fully clothed, she slept sprawled across her bed all night.

The next day, in a state of shock but forcing themselves to do what had to be done, Rosa and Nora sat at the dining room table and worked on the funeral program.

Grandpa William was in a fog and of no help in making Grandma Lilly's funeral arrangements. William could not eat of his own volition. He had to be force fed by Nora, Douglas, and Rosa—mostly by Douglas and Rosa. After the few meals he was forced to eat, William returned to his bedroom and sat alone, grieving over the loss of his wife to whom he had been married for nearly fifty years.

Meanwhile, Rosa and Nora pored over mementos, old church bulletins and newspaper clippings, and college and sorority tributes to glean information necessary to write Lilly Johnson's obituary. A couple of days later, Rosa accompanied her mother to the funeral home to select a coffin and speak with the director about flowers, funeral cars needed, and burial arrangements. On the same day, they talked with the pastor of their church about the funeral service. Rosa remained at her mother's side every step of the way, helping to make necessary phone calls, writing letters, and sending obituary information and photographs to the Colored newspaper. All of this Rosa did while in a stunned frame of mind. Her thoughts on the finality of death gripped her. That she would never see her grandmother alive again weighed on her. And yet it was a relief for her to know she would not have to think about having or not having Grandma Lilly's approval on anything ever again.

At the funeral, in a black suit, William appeared sedated. Beside him, and also in black, was Nora crying silently, her body heaving gently at times, as tears streamed down her cheeks. To Nora's right was Douglas, in a navy blue suit, holding Nora's hand. To Douglas's right, in a white dress, Dot cried audibly. Beside her, Willie sat stoned and red-eyed presumably from both alcohol and tears of grief. Not paying attention to her immediate family seated to her left, Rosa, in a black dress with a white collar, sat with a somber face. Aside from feeling guilt over having wished death and hell on Grandma Lilly for not accepting her for who she was and for whom she was becoming, Rosa felt as if her grandmother's death marked the end of an era and a new beginning. Then, wondering what it was going to mean for her family, she glanced to her left and looked at each of them.

Nora now sat slumped and red-faced, with tear-smudged make-up and a look of hopeless abandonment. Douglas was still holding Nora's hand. His face was solemn but he did not appear grief stricken. Dot whimpered audibly, with tears streaming down her make-up free face. Her light-brown pompadour hairstyle was in slight disarray. Willie was looking down at his hands.

As the immediate family and other relatives and close friends sat in somberness and grief, the choir sang hymns and readers read scriptures. A few of Lilly's life-long friends offered tributes. The pastor delivered the eulogy. Finally, the casket was opened one last time; so that the family and then others could view the body before the recessional and journey to the cemetery.

*   *   *   *

After leaving the cemetery, family and friends returned to the church. They filtered into the social hall, a huge room off from the sanctuary. The room was lined with baskets of colorful flowers. Buffet tables were on the left side of the room and several churchwomen stood behind them ready to serve members of the family, their friends, and others in attendance. As people filed alongside the tables, picked up plates and were served, a pianist in a far corner of the room played soft popular and semi-sacred music.

All who wanted to eat were served their choice of foods: collard greens, corn on the cob, green beans and boiled potatoes, baked and fried chicken, mashed potatoes, cabbage, ham, potato salad, tossed salad, rolls and cornbread. The choices also included slices of a variety of cakes and pies. Tea, fruit punch, and coffee were the available drinks.

After being served, the people sat at white cloth-covered tables in the center of the great room and settled into eating and conversing. Many attendees renewed contact with old friends and associates they had not seen in years. Some acknowledged that it took a funeral to reunite them, as funerals and weddings tend to do. As time and good food drew them further into socializing, a steady hum of conversation filled the room.

After dinner, friends and associates offered parting words to the family, and soon the crowd dispersed. The family then re-entered designated funeral cars and were transported back to Summit Place. Once they arrived at the house, William's attorney, Thomas McMillan, assembled the family around the dining room table for the reading of Lilly Johnson's will.

Lilly bequeathed to William and Nora money from her life insurance policies. She left William fifty thousand dollars from a policy she had fulfilled during the many years she had taught school. Her share of the house also went to William.

To Nora Lilly left twenty thousand dollars, her valuable jewelry, plus her china, silverware, and an expensive cedar chest.

To Willie, Grandmother Lilly left three thousand dollars in cash, to be parceled to him at his mother's discretion.

From some investments that had paid off for Lilly, she left a generous trust fund for Dot, which once Dot turned twenty-one years old would pay her each month for the rest of her life.

To Rosa, Lilly left nothing.

Rosa was stunned that she was the only grandchild to whom Lilly had left no legacy at all. Tears glazed her eyes. She pulled a handkerchief from the small purse on her lap and feigned the need to blow her nose, so she could dab her eyes and keep the angry tears from streaming down her face. She hoped her face did not reveal the pain she felt at the final blow her grandmother had dealt her. Rosa would never understand why Lilly had not been able to love her. How could her dark skin and determination to fulfill her own dream with the kind of music she loved most make her grandmother hate her so?

Douglas too was angry that Lilly had left Rosa out of her will. Trying to cheer Rosa after the lawyer left the house, Douglas said, "Don't worry about it, baby. The old witch didn't mention me in her will either."

Rosa looked at her father. "Well, there was never any love lost between you and Grandma Lilly anyway, you know?" Rosa then blew her nose. "But then again, what's Mama's is yours."

"Yeah, but I wouldn't touch a penny of what she left your mother."

"I don't see how you can avoid it over time. Mama's not a selfish person."

Douglas put his arm around Rosa's shoulder. "Hey, with all the talent you've got, you don't need anything from anybody," he said. "You can make your own wealth in this world, and on your own terms."

Neither Douglas nor Rosa complained to Nora about Lilly leaving Rosa out of her will. They knew Nora was filled with grief, and they respected that.

For the next several days, their local family, friends, and fellow church members streamed in and out of the Johnson, Stills home. They delivered pans of hot food, bowls of salad, platters of cold sliced meats and cheeses, fruit, breads, soft drinks, coffee, tea, and napkins. Additionally they brought toiletries: soaps, shampoos, deodorants, and detergents. This display of sympathy and love was so overwhelming that it kept Nora's and Williams' eyes filled with tears. Douglas, Rosa, and Rosa's friend Elsie accepted the food and other items and placed them in the kitchen and the dining room. In order to protect Nora and William during their early grieving period, the trio screened visitors who might talk to them too long.

Nora and William seemed oblivious to the approaching holiday season. And so did everyone else in Rosa's immediate family. Rosa doubted that either Thanksgiving or Christmas, especially Christmas, would ever be normal for the maternal side of her family again. Grandma Lilly had always made the most fuss over Christmas, and now she was gone. How ironic it was that the person who had been the greatest complainer in their home all year except at Christmas Time should take with her to the grave the family's usual merriment during that special season.

Rosa mused that Christmas might never be exciting in their home again, unless Willie or Dot were to marry and have children. A new generation of small children without a Grandma Lilly in their daily lives would afford the Johnson, Stills home the opportunity to have a Christmas-like spirit in the house all year round.

Rosa saw little chance of herself becoming a mother. Although she loved family and children, she did not feel the need to birth any babies herself. And although Rosa believed that one day she would have a man of her own in her life, she did not feel it would be necessary to have babies from that union. Babies would not fit into her career. Her love of children would have to be satisfied by her future nieces and nephews.

Rosa waited another couple of weeks before leaving for New York. When the time came, she left D.C. with her father's blessing and the assurance that he would take care of her mother. Along with Douglas's blessing came a word of caution.

. "Now, baby, I know you've kept up with the news stories on how the Government is cracking down on celebrities involved in Communism, right?" he said.

"Yes, Papa, I have," Nora replied.

"Well just be careful not to get involved with any actor, writer, singer, or anybody else who might be a Communist. The Federal Government is investigating and locking up communists and people who even look like they might be communists.

"Papa, you have my word. I always observe people first. I never make fast friends, you know?"

"That's my girl," Douglas answered.

"I'm not even going to become friends with communist *sympathizers*.

I've got too much at stake. I refuse to let anything jeopardize my career."

Once Rosa reassured her father she would be all right, and she was reassured that both her parents were totally supportive of her and would be okay in her absence, she was set. She did not need Willie's or Dot's approval or good wishes. Willie would live his own life and so would Dot. Rosa had a career to begin.

PART II

▼

CHAPTER 24

▼

New York City
January 1950

In New York, Rosa rented an apartment in Harlem. A few days later she picked up a used beige sedan she had agreed to buy from a Harlem resident and Howard University alumnus a few years her senior. Once she started the paperwork that would change the vehicle into her name, she drove around Harlem and other neighborhoods, off and on for about a week, acquainting herself with the City. The next week she drove downtown to The Blue Phoenix, the night club on 52nd Street, where she had recently secured her first New York gig. Rosa went back to the club a couple more afternoons and practiced with the band. At the end of the next week, she started singing fulltime at the club.

On her first night as a fulltime singer, Rosa was stunning in an ivory-colored form-fitting dress and matching satin high heels. The neckline of her dress was just low enough to show the promise of voluptuousness. Her jeweled earrings and choker completed the outfit. As an added touch, Rosa wore a silk crimson rose in her upswept hair, just above her right ear.

As she glided onto the stage and took her place in front of the microphone, the band played an introduction to *Our Love Is Here To Stay*.

Rosa neared her lips to the microphone, opened her mouth, let gentle breaths caress it, and then started singing slowly in her rich mellow tone, "It's…ve-ry-y…clear…our love is here…to stay-y-y." From this slow and deliberate beginning, she moved the song to a moderate tempo, while raising her arms and snapping her fingers to the beat she controlled. With improvisation, she commanded the stage and enraptured the audience. On the second verse, she did some scat singing and weaving in and out, becoming an instrument along with the trumpet players and saxophonists, causing the band and the audience to fall madly in love with her and her vocal style.

Amidst thunderous applause, Rosa bowed, took a calming breath, and gracefully outstretched an arm towards the band, acknowledging their importance to her exciting performance.

The image of poise, she walked to the piano at the side of the stage, sat down, and re-adjusted the microphone atop the piano. Rosa placed her palms on her lap a moment, then raised her hands to the keyboard and began playing *September Song*. At times she leaned towards the mike, or pulled her head back slowly from it, as the mood dictated. Other times, she leaned from side to side as she moved her fingers along the keys, and maneuvered her voice from the lowest to the highest notes in its amazing range.

Rosa sang and played, making love to the music, becoming one with the song. Her performance rendered her adorable to the audience. Singing a variety of upbeat songs and ballads, she performed three sets, and the club's patrons begged for more; so she did a fourth set that night. As a result, her audience was hooked. They spread the word, and the club was filled on every night Rosa performed there.

After appearing at The Blue Phoenix for a couple of months, she met Jackson Parker, owner of a restaurant in Harlem. His friends called him by his last name, and he invited Rosa to do the same. They swept each other into an affair, which Rosa held onto, in case it turned out that Alan really did get married. Rosa liked Parker and enjoyed her sexual relationship with him.

Parker sometimes asked Rosa if she loved him. She never responded directly to that question. Instead she skirted around it. "Parker, I'm not like a lot of other women, so don't expect me to be, okay? Don't expect me to be drooling all over you, because you look good and know how to make a woman feel good in bed."

"Well, it would be nice to hear it once in a while," Parker said. "You know what I'm sayin', baby?"

"Sure I do. But I'm just not one of those 'I love you, love you, love you' kind of women. So don't be asking me that anymore, okay honey? Give me a break from that, all right? A long break."

Parker honored Rosa's request. However, he still showed her he liked her broad smile, her sexiness, her talent and style, her earthiness. She was hot and very sensuous, he reminded her more than a few times.

But soon Parker told Rosa he did not want her flirting with band members at the club or with men anywhere else for that matter. He started acting possessive of her. He appeared territorial whenever they walked down the street together. He waited outside the rear door of the club at night and whenever he saw a man look at her, he put his arm around her and pulled her close, or held her hand and would not let it go until they entered his shiny black chrysler. If he saw her talking with a strange man, he interrogated her about it. She tolerated his possessiveness for a while, mainly because there was no other man in New York who captured her attention.

CHAPTER 25

▼

February 1950

Rosa did not have to go to rehearsal, and yet she did not feel like staying indoors all day. Deciding around noon to go out, she bathed and pulled on some clothes.

With a rust-colored felt hat on her head and bundled in a black wool coat with a brown fur collar, Rosa strutted for several blocks under a gray sky to *Jackson's Café*, and popped in on Parker unexpectedly.

A uniformed waitress was taking lunch orders from the few customers at the counter. Parker was in the kitchen overseeing the cook and the servers. They were preparing orders for current patrons, as well as food for the dinner crowd who would stroll in later, in the evening, and sit at the several square tables out on the floor.

Rosa sat at the counter rather than taking a seat at one of the tables. A waitress appeared from the kitchen and took her order, a fried chicken sandwich and a cup of hot tea. The waitress then strode back into the kitchen.

Rosa took off her coat and laid it on the bar stool next to her. She smoothed the hair above her ears and patted the twisted hair at the back of her neck. Her green skirt and sweater were smooth, and the sheer stockings and brown shoes were impeccable.

While waiting for her food and expecting Parker to exit the kitchen and notice she was there, Rosa sat and peered around the restaurant. She glanced at the tables, a newspaper stand, a jukebox, and a public telephone. On a closed door in a distant corner she saw a sign that said *Restrooms*. The restaurant's walls were pale green and displayed several framed and autographed black-and-white photos of jazz musicians who had eaten there. Also on the walls were a couple of large drawings: one of a jazz quartet, another of a trim saxophonist, and still another showed a hefty trumpet player. On the wall behind the counter, leading to the kitchen, was a horizontal menu.

Having surveyed the room, Rosa looked up just as Parker was coming out of the kitchen towards the counter. His face lit up. "Well hi young lady! What brings you here? Don't get me wrong, it's a nice surprise," he said, smiling at her.

"Oh, I just wanted to get out of the apartment for a while. Wanted to change my routine of rehearsing all afternoon or napping, or just staying in until time to go to The Blue Phoenix"

"Okay! Well. I'm glad to be the benefactor of you breaking the monotony in your routine today."

They continued exchanging light banter, as a slender, medium brown-skinned woman entered the restaurant. After spotting Parker talking with Rosa, the woman stopped in her tracks.

Parker looked up and saw the slender woman. "Hey, Belle, how're you doing?" he asked

Rosa spun half around on her bar stool, so she could see who Parker was addressing.

"The question is how are *you* doing?" Belle answered. "Or better yet, *who* are you doing it *with*?"

"Come on over and meet Rosa," Parker said, ignoring Belle's apparent innuendo. "This is Rosa Stills. She's a new singer at The Blue Phoenix," Parker added.

Rosa was about to smile and say glad to meet you, but Belle prevented her.

"Am I supposed to be impressed or something?" Belle said, sharply.

"Well you'd be impressed if you heard this lady sing," Parker said firmly with a half smile"

"Yeah, well, I'm not interested in what she does for a livin'. To get right to the point, I just wanna know if she's sleepin' witch you."

Rosa turned around to face the bar. She placed her hands on the bar and clasped them, not saying a word, not looking at Parker or anyone else.

A few customers at the bar, two young men in wool jackets, blue work shirts and dark khakis, and a middle-aged woman in a gray coat and blue dress, looked curiously at Belle and Parker.

"Whether she is or is not is my business, not yours, Belle. Now if you wanna eat or have a beer, sit your ass down, and I'll have somebody bring you what you want," he said coldly, as he turned around and stepped towards the kitchen.

Belle sat down beside Rosa and gave her a glance, which, if looks could kill, would have disposed of Rosa forever.

Unafraid, yet not wanting to remain during the unpleasantness she could tell was not over, Rosa pulled her coat from the bar stool on her other side. She then stood and, in a tone loud enough for Parker to hear, said, "Parker! I just remembered I've got an appointment. I don't have time to eat after all."

He reappeared from the kitchen. "You leaving, baby? You don't have to go. Ain't no body here got ties on me. This is my joint. Stay and eat. Food's ready."

But with her coat and hat already on, Rosa said, "Thanks, Parker, but I've got to go and talk to my manager. See you later." She strode confidently towards the door.

Belle looked at her with venomous eyes. "It betta be much later, like never. Parker is *my* man, you got that?"

Parker shot Belle a hard look.

Rosa strode out of the restaurant without looking back.

Later that night, after Rosa had left The Blue Phoenix and was in her apartment winding down from the performance energy she still felt, she heard a knock on her door.

Rosa knew Alan would never come to see her that late. Neither would her new friends or any of the band members stop by that time of night; which was actually the wee hours of the morning. She knew it could be only one person: Parker. Wearing a pink satin night gown and matching robe, Rosa opened the door with a matter of fact look on her face. "I knew it was you," she said. "I told you about coming this late to see me. What's wrong with the daylight hours, Parker? I'm not saying real early, cause I'll just be getting to sleep good. I'm talking about in the afternoon, something civilized. You know what I mean? Does any of what I'm saying make sense to you?"

"Yeah, yeah, it does. But now that I'm heah, you gon let me in or what?" he said with one foot in the living room.

"Seems to me you're already inside," she said, walking away from him. "And I don't feel like trying to push you out, so. Whatever." She sat on the dark green armchair, and resumed sipping a glass of wine.

"You gon' offer me a drink?" he asked, standing before her in a navy blue pinstripe suit.

"Wine's on the kitchen counter. Help yourself."

"I knew I shoulda brought some real liquor with me," he said. "But since I didn't, I'll make do with whatcha got here." In the kitchen, Parker poured himself a glass of wine and returned to the living room. He sat on the sofa facing her.

"To us," he said, as he held the glass in the air a moment. He then gulped down a third of his wine.

"What're you doing here, Parker? I'm not your woman. We're just friends."

"We might be just friends right now, but I'm gon' make you my woman. I'm gon' be so good to you, you're not gon' want anybody but me."

"Hm-hm. Yeah, we'll see," she said.

He gulped down the remainder of his wine and sat the glass on the lamp table next to the sofa.

Rosa, sitting with her legs crossed and her pink satin robe half open had already placed her glass on the lamp table next to the chair in which she sat. She was pulling her hair back away from her face, and breathing in deeply, feeling the bit of relaxation the wine afforded her.

Parker stood and walked over to her. He then reached down and took Rosa's hand in his. He pulled her gently from her seat. And once she was standing before him, he smiled his approval of her sexy appearance in the negligee and matching robe she modeled. He encircled her waist with his arms, pulling her firmly against his body. He leaned down and turned her face toward his, kissed her urgently, and began walking her towards the bedroom.

Why not? she thought. *If he's really going to treat me as good as he claims he will, he might just inspire me to give Alan back to pathetic little Iris.*

CHAPTER 26

▼

March 1950

Rosa's Washington, D.C. contacts kept her abreast of news about Alan, and they informed her that he did in fact marry Iris. The wedding details they provided to her were like jagged-edged daggers piercing, gouging, and then ripping out her heart. Yet an intense curiosity holding her in its grip would not allow Rosa to silence her informers.

They told her that Alan and Iris were married at Capital Episcopal Church, in Washington, with 300 guests from New York, Memphis, Atlanta, Detroit, and Philadelphia in attendance. Tuxedoed ushers escorted the bride's mother, in a lacy mauve dress and the groom's mother, in gold satin, down the isle to the front pews on their respective family's sides of the sanctuary.

Soon the tall to medium-height ushers, in an array of skin colors from high yellow to medium brown and displaying varying degrees of good facial features and physiques, escorted well-dressed family and friends down the long aisle and led them to pews on the appropriate sides of the sanctuary.

While the congregation waited for the ceremony to begin, musicians played organ and piano music, and three soloists sang. A reed-like man with pale yellow skin stood tall in a black suit and sang the popular wedding song, *Because*, in a beautiful tenor voice. A willowy, pink-skinned lyric soprano in a long black skirt and white blouse sang the song, *I Love You Truly*, and a matronly olive-hued contralto in a long navy blue dress sang *The Lord's Prayer*.

As an interlude, a light brown-skinned harpist in a black formal length dress played Johann Pachelbel's *Canon in D*.

Soon afterwards, the organist began playing *The Wedding March*, and twelve bridesmaids in long, bright green dresses, coupled with twelve groomsmen in black tuxedoes, began their procession down the aisle. One junior bridesmaid in a pastel green dress, escorted by a junior groomsman in a black tuxedo followed behind. Two four-year-old boys in off-white suits, and each holding a small satin pillow with a gold ring fastened on top, followed the junior attendants. Three little girls in cream-colored dresses processed down the aisle at a slower pace, strewing variegated flower petals along their way.

Once the bridal party reached the altar, the organist ceased playing for a moment, and then started playing chords, signaling the beginning of *The Bridal March*. The congregation stood. And then Iris Haywood, her face veiled by white lace and her slender body dressed in a white satin gown with a trailing lace train, began her measured walk with her father down the aisle towards the altar. Waiting there for her, along with the bridal party, were the church's gray-haired, black-robed minister and her husband to be. Alan Covington stood erect and looked serious in a black tuxedo with tails, white shirt and charcoal-colored bow tie. His identically dressed, olive skinned best man stood at his side.

The reception was held in the church's large fellowship hall. After photos were taken, the receiving line greeted what seemed like an interminable stream of guests. Afterwards, everyone was treated to a formal dinner with waiters serving an elaborate menu and tuxedoed musicians playing music by Duke Ellington, Benny Goodman, and George Gershwin. Amid a hum of light and steady conversation, the band played popular music. Soon the band leader silenced the musicians; so that toasts to the bride and groom could be offered. The best man and close friends of the groom told humorous stories. Everyone enjoyed a first class meal with drinks and later dessert. While family, friends, and other guests were eating and chatting above the sound of live music and the tinkle of champagne glasses, the bride and groom slipped out of the church and into a limousine, and then headed away for their honeymoon.

The newlyweds reportedly honeymooned in Rome, Italy.

In addition to hearing accounts of the wedding and reception from friends and associates, Rosa also read accounts of the big event in the society pages of the *Amsterdam News,* New York City's Colored newspaper, and in clippings from the *Washington Afro-American*, which Elsie mailed to her. For weeks following the news, Rosa was sad and filled with pain that *she* was not Alan's bride.

CHAPTER 27

▼

1950

Over the months, newspapers, radio and television announced a number of astounding events. Some happened before Alan and Iris's spring wedding some happened afterwards. The astounding events included January 15: four thousand delegates from one hundred national organizations attended the National Emergency Civil Rights Conference in Washington, D.C.; May 1: Poet Gwendolyn Brooks was the first black recipient of a Pulitzer Prize, for her poetry book titled *Annie Allen*; June 28: Actor, Singer and Civil Rights Activist Paul Robeson called on President Truman to stop sending troops, especially black soldiers to the war in Korea.

As the world turned, Rosa Johnson Stills was making a name for herself as a jazz singer by drawing crowds into New York City's noted nightclub, The Blue Phoenix.

Even as Rosa focused on her performances at The Blue Phoenix, she made time to stay in touch with Elsie in order to keep up with Alan and Iris. She also received updates on Elsie's family and her own family. Sometimes she would ask if Elsie had seen Willie or heard anything about him and Dot, just to get a perspective on them from someone other than Douglas and Nora.

Rosa learned that Elsie's family was okay. Elsie and her husband were struggling, and sometimes he would get discouraged, but she knew they were going to make it. They would be all right, Elsie said, because they wanted to be independent of their parents and they loved each other.

Elsie informed Rosa that she had run into Willie and learned that Willie—although he had been in counseling in an effort to stay sober—had relapsed. He had skipped meetings and gone on drinking binges. He told Elsie he felt like an old man. His father was angry with him, so he did not go to Summit Place much, and when he did it was when he knew his father was not at home.

Dot, Elsie said, was still the social butterfly. She was dating different boys and was both the most popular and the most envied of all her girlfriends; because all the boys wanted her, and because she was the prettiest and the best dressed girl in her crowd.

Rosa made sure Elsie had her New York address and phone number and asked Elsie to keep her updated on Willie and Dot. Especially Willie. Willie was the weaker of her siblings, but he was the best, Rosa said.

Elsie promised to keep Rosa informed.

Always during their phone talks, Rosa told Elsie about how things were going at The Blue Phoenix and how much she enjoyed working there. She also confided in Elsie concerning her unchanged feelings for Alan.

Elsie mainly listened. She rarely offered direct advice. Instead she asked Rosa questions like, "Do you think he'll ever leave Iris?" Or "What do you think is really keeping him with Iris?" Or, "If you had your wish and Alan divorced Iris, where would you two live? Do you think your career would be affected in any way, especially if Alan wanted to have children with you?"

Those were the kinds of questions Rosa would sometimes answer and other times avoid by saying, "Hey, Elsie, I've got to go to rehearsal now." Or she'd say, "Someone's at the door. Let me talk to you later, okay?"

CHAPTER 28

▼

New York City
September 1950

After six months of what Iris and outsiders thought was wedded bliss, Alan's work took him to New York for several days. He traveled by train and arrived on a Friday evening. Carrying only a small travel bag, he was able to go from the station directly to The Blue Phoenix.

Because Alan was light enough to pass for white, he entered the club through the front door and sat at one of the tables with the white audience. After Rosa finished her last set, Alan waited for her outside, in the rear of the club, where she was required to exit; because she was obviously Colored. Not knowing he was in New York and waiting for her outside the club, Rosa was shocked to see him. They did not publicly display their happiness at seeing one another. However, their eyes expressed the love they still felt for each other. After a long moment of embracing each other with their eyes only, the two headed to Rosa's apartment.

As soon as they walked inside and closed her apartment door, Rosa unbuttoned Alan's shirt and pulled it off of him. She raised his undershirt, laid her face against his hairy chest, and then began kissing his chest, as he planted kisses down her neck while pulling her dress up her legs and over her hips. She helped him ease out of his undershirt. He finished undressing her. She led him to the bedroom; where she lay on the bed, on her back, and beckoned to him to join her. Instead of mounting her, he turned her over so that her stomach was against the mattress, and then straddled her and began massaging her shoulders.

"Where's your lotion," he asked, gently working his magical hands downwards on her back.

"On the nightstand, right there. Can you reach it?"

"Yes," he said, stretching his arm to retrieve the bottle.

He poured some in his hand, then recapped the bottle and dropped it on the carpet. His massage relaxed her, making her even more eager for his next move. He kissed the back of her neck, shoulders, upper back, the small of her back and buttocks. As he began to part her legs, she said, "Wait a minute, baby," and turned over and climbed on top of him. She nibbled his ear, moved to his face, giving him urgent wet kisses, then moved to his neck, down to his chest, his stomach, and down, down.

"Ah-h-h…umh-h-h, he uttered, exhaling heavily, sighing with the pleasure he felt. Ooh-hh.

She drove him to frenzy, until he arched his back and then sank onto the sheets.

She stretched out and lay on her back, beside him. After several moments, he rose and straddled her, and kissed her face slowly, then her neck, downward to her breasts, loving each one in turn, stirring her juices again. He kissed her stomach, pelvic area, then opened his mouth and began tasting her fruit, probing, partaking of her juice, her deliciousness, until she peaked, and her soul screamed his name. He slowly released her and lay on his back. They were still for a while. And then Rosa aroused him again. She began a joyous ride, taking him with her to exciting places, high, then higher, and higher to a state of ecstasy. She leaned her body forward, stretched her thighs and legs backwards the full length of his legs, so they could reach the mountaintop together, tensing, easing, sliding on the sweat, the oil, the juice, tensing together, releasing, silently shouting each others names, deeply exhaling, slowly sinking into the sheets into contentment, and ultimately falling asleep together.

The next morning, Alan awoke with Rosa in his arms. He had a sheepish grin on his face. Rosa smiled and kissed him gently on the lips. He closed the space between their naked bodies, and they made love again. Afterwards he closed his eyes and drifted back to sleep. Rosa then slipped out of bed. After brushing her teeth and bathing, she cooked breakfast. Just before she placed the food on the table, she padded to the bedroom and looked in on Alan. Seeing that he was awake, she announced, "Breakfast is ready."

"I know. Smells delicious." He said. "Let me get a shower, and I'll be right there."

"No. Just brush your teeth and come on and eat while it's hot," she said. "Take a shower later."

"Okay," he replied. "You're the boss, Boss."

"Uhm, hmm," she uttered with a smile, as she left the bedroom and headed towards the kitchen.

While they were eating breakfast, Rosa told Alan she wished they could relocate to Paris together. She was sure she could find work in a club there. He could get work there too, she added. They would be happy in Paris. She was convinced of it, judging from her friends' accounts of their visits and times living there, and also from the stories her parents had shared with her about Paris. They would be far from the racism they faced in the States, she told him.

Alan dreamed along with Rosa for a while, but before he left to return to D.C., he told her he would have to see. "Leaving my marriage won't be easy," he said. "It's not going to be easy leaving the law firm either," he said. "I've proven myself to be a valuable attorney for the firm. But I'll try to think of a way to work it all out," he promised

Each day of that week, Alan took care of his legal business during the day; had dinner with Rosa in the evening, and made love to her all night. On the weekend he ate at the club. When Rosa got off work and they returned to her apartment, she simply ate something light before they made love and fell asleep in each other's arms.

Alan acted on his obvious intoxication with Rosa's beauty, her body, and her love. He acted as if he had been marooned on an island for the previous six months and was just now able to be with another human being, a truly loving person. He seemed as if he had been hungering for the kind of physical attention Rosa gave him; the way she kissed him, touched and stroked him, the way her hands moved in his erogenous areas. He responded to her lovemaking and to her company as if she possessed unlimited insight into his soul.

Rosa knew she had Alan's love, for that had for so many years been her aim, her focus outside of her singing career. But his commitment to what his and Iris's family wanted for him—a loveless marriage—was beyond her understanding.

What will it take to break that hold they have over Alan? Rosa pondered. *I'm going to think of SOMETHING, because I'm definitely going to break it.*

CHAPTER 29

▼

Washington, D.C.
September 1950

After he returned home, Alan acted differently. He seemed distracted whenever Iris talked to him. When they were in bed at night he was distant and did not want to make love to her. He feigned a headache or fatigue or simply turned his back to her and remained that way all night.

Whenever he and Iris did make love, she initiated it and insisted that he finish the act. Afterwards, he withdrew to his side of the bed, and did not let his body touch her for the rest of the night. When she mentioned his cold behavior the next morning, or at some other opportune time, he shrugged it off. Because she would not accept his behavior as all in her mind, they began to argue. She accused him of having an affair. Alan denied it and was always on the defensive when she brought up the subject.

Iris reacted to Alan's defensive stance with even more suspicion and insecurity. She began to rifle through his brief case, luggage, and snooped in his pants and coat pockets. When their phone bill arrived, she scrutinized it. And whenever the phone rang, she made sure she was the one who answered it. However, Alan seemed careful not to leave concrete evidence that Iris could discover and use against him.

He knew that although Iris would never leave him, she would enjoy having hard evidence to prove her suspicions were correct whenever she started her verbal attacks against him. She had done that a few times in the past, during a couple of meaningless flings he had had with women other than Rosa. But she had never been able to prove his affair with Rosa. Even though friends of hers had buzzed about it, and even though her intuition told her it was happening.

Though she possessed no concrete evidence, Iris must have known in her heart that she had always shared Alan with Rosa. From high school on, whenever the three of them had been in the same room at a fundraiser or other event, the sexual tension between Alan and Rosa had been palpable. And whenever Rosa was circulating and working the crowd faraway from Alan and Iris, Alan always seemed to end up near Rosa. At times, the two would end up together across the room from Iris or out on the porch or patio. When that happened, Iris would find them, and inevitably tell Alan there was someone waiting to meet him or talk with him. Or she would fabricate some other reason to pull him away from Rosa. As she did so, Iris sometimes gave Rosa a syrupy but sarcastic look that said: *No, sweetie, you'll never really have him.*

CHAPTER 30

▼

New York
September 1950

Parker noticed Rosa was different. He was suspicious and claimed Rosa even smelled different.

"What do you care how I smell, as long as it's not a bad odor? And what difference does it make where I go or what I do, or with whom? Don't you do whatever you want? And with whomever you want? You think I don't know what's going on, Parker?"

"What're you talking about, woman?"

"I'm talking about that whore who's always hanging around you at the café. That skinny woman with the straw-looking hair and makeup so thick you could scrape it off her face. *Belle*, or whatever her name is. You know the one I'm talking about. Don't play dumb, Parker."

"Oh, you're talkin' about Belle Hudson. Yeah. Well, she don't mean nothin' to me. She ain't got nothin' goin' for her."

"Yeah, try telling *her* that," Rosa said, rotating her head with her hands on her hips. "I heard that woman is so evil and insecure, that you can't even glance at another woman without her getting loud and accusing you of sleeping with the woman. I also heard she acts the same way when she sees another woman smile at you or even look at you longer than two seconds."

"Look here, Rosa, I told you she don't mean nothin' to me, and she don't. Now that's the end of it. It's none of your business anyway."

"Yeah, well I'm making it my business. If you can come in here and tell me who I should and shouldn't see, and threaten me, then I can get in your business, too."

"Watch your mouth now," Parker warned.

"I can say whatever I want to say. This is my place. I can do and say what I please in here. If you don't like it, you can leave!" She said, her voice rising.

Parker pushed her.

She nearly lost her balance.

He pushed her again, towards the bedroom. In the bedroom he threw her on the bed and forced himself on her, into her. He used his manhood as a weapon as he brutally took her, jabbing himself into her mercilessly as if showing her that he was the boss.

"Get off me, Parker. Get off! NOW!" Rosa shouted, beating his arms and back with her fists.

"Is it mine?" he asked, still jabbing inside of her.

"Yeah, now get OFF me, damn it!"

Again he demanded to know, "Is it mine? ALL mine?" Say it so I can HEAH you.

"Yeah, yeah, Parker. YEAH! Now get off me. Please, Parker, you're hurting me. You're hurting me real bad. Please get off me."

As if her pleading excited him to a climax, he exploded inside her, and then rolled off her and over to the other side of the bed, breathing heavily.

It was the first time Rosa had been raped. Feeling sore inside, she rose slowly from the bed and dragged herself out of the room and into the bathroom. She sat on the toilet first, wanting to let his abusive liquid drain from her. Afterwards, she rose from the toilet and took a warm shower quickly, hoping he would not enter the bathroom, while she washed his smell, his musk, his liquids, his presence from her body.

Upon stepping out of the shower, Rosa dried her body with a towel, pulled on a yellow robe, then went back into the bedroom and put on her clothes, keeping her eye on him as she did so.

Parker did not bother to shower but dressed himself quietly. It was evident to him that Rosa was angry as well as hurt. He broke the silence. "You all right?"

"As if you care." She said solemnly, as she pulled her stockings up her legs and over her thighs.

"You know I care about you, baby. It's just that I go crazy at the thought of you with another man, and—"

"—What makes you think I was with another man?" she asked coldly, attaching the tops of her stockings to the garters hanging from her white garter belt, down her thighs. "And whether I was or not," she said, raising her voice, "you have no right to RAPE me!"

"I know, baby, but sometimes you just drive me crazy. I mean as good and sexy as you look…as talented as you are. I see the way those guys in the band look at you. And I know you're respectable around them. But I'm thinking, what if one o' those guys could move in on me. One o' them or even one o' the guys you know back in D.C.," he said, his eyes pleading for her to understand his view-point.

"I don't care what you might be thinking or feeling. That's no excuse for you to handle me the way you did just now. You treated me like you hate me, like you hate all women!"

"No, baby, it ain't like that. I won't do it like that anymore, not just on inse-curity, anyway." Then his face turned demonic looking. "But if I ever actually catch you with somebody—in bed, I mean—I *will* have to mess you up. Even if I see you with a man and it looks to me like you really with him that way, I'll *mess* you up. And I'll probably have to *kill* him."

Parker's threatening statement instantly caused Rosa to know she was going to make plans to leave New York. She could not remain involved with a man with a penchant for violence.

Parker then softened his tone. "But I know I'll never have to do that, right?"

"Right," she said, in order to appease him and, she hoped, keep him from harming her further.

"Now come' ere," he said pulling her to him.

She hugged him, feigning pleasure at making up with him, even though she was nervous and felt at that moment like she hated him. She knew she would have to be extra careful during Alan's next visit to New York.

It wasn't until a few days later that Rosa felt the full impact of Parker's physi-cal abuse of her. Her inner thighs and genitals were sore and a burning sensation seared her female organs and urinal tract. Because of the pain, she called in and asked The Blue Phoenix owner-manager for time off, telling him she had a severe sore throat and actually could not sing for a few days. He allowed Rosa time off, saying he could let a couple of local singers fill in while she was out.

A few days turned into more than a week. Just when Rosa thought the sore-ness and burning had dissipated and she felt relief for a day, the condition recurred and became worse. Urinating was painful, searing the nerves of her uri-nary tract and knifing pain upwards into her stomach and under her breasts. She vowed to kill a man before she would let him treat her body like that again. She would keep a knife or some sharp weapon near the bed, so if a man turned out to be crazy and refused to get off her at her command, she would seriously injure him and definitely leave her mark on his body.

Rosa nursed herself by sitting in warm baths, soaking, resting, eating chicken soup and drinking hot tea and fruit juices.

The thought of calling the police and filing a rape report crossed her mind, but since she had let him into her apartment, the rape charge probably would not stick, she figured. If she had known Parker would treat a woman that violently in bed, she never would have gotten involved with him in the first place. Now that it had happened, she vowed never to get in bed with him again.

Nearly two weeks went by before Rosa felt totally healed. She then returned to work. The club owner, the band, and her audience were wildly pleased to have her back, as evidenced by their thundering applause and verbal adulation after she completed her first set.

Among those who came to greet her was an unfamiliar face in the band, a stand-in for their regular trumpet player. The stand-in trumpeter hung back until most of the club's patrons had their moments with her. Just before she started to walk towards the back, to her dressing room, he approached her. A tall, dark brown-skinned, middle-aged man, he had a brilliant smile that revealed what Rosa thought were nice white teeth for his age. His thick shiny eyebrows and mustache bore no gray strands. But there was a patch of gray hair at each temple. The trumpet player took her hand and kissed it. "You're a great talent, young lady. And you're a wonderful song stylist." He reached into the pocket of his suit jacket and brought out a calling card, which he placed in her hand. "Give me a call when you're free. We can talk and I'll steer you to some connections that can help further your career. Have you performed in Europe yet? Ever sing at any jazz spots in Paris?"

If I were light-skinned, I'd be turning red right now, Rosa thought, feeling goose bumps on her arms and a fluttering in her stomach over the unexpected encounter. *Is this man just flirting with me, or is he genuinely admiring my talent and really able to help me?*

"No, I haven't been out of the States yet," Rosa replied. "This is the first job I've had where I'm the headliner. Have you worked in Paris?" she asked.

"Yeah, over twenty years ago," the trumpet player said. "I know some American musicians who're over there now. Some of them were over there when I was there and just stayed. Some go over to do a gig, stay for a while, and then come back home. There's nothing like it. You should put Paris in your plans. The

French jazz lovers would adore you and your style. And a European experience would elevate your reputation as an artist after you come back to the States."

"I'll keep that in mind," Rosa said, taking in the trumpeter's good looks and still wondering what his intentions might be. Although he was a handsome man, who had probably been gorgeous in his day, she felt an affinity for him that was not at all sexual. It was as if she had known him before, but did not know where she had met him or otherwise been in his presence. In a moment, she shrugged off those feelings, thinking they had probably come to her simply because he was an artist. She glanced down at his card and did not recognize the name on it. She had one last question for him.

"Do you think you'll ever go back to Paris?" she asked.

"No, no. Paris was good for me when I was young, and it served its purpose in those days. But at my age, I don't want to be that far away from my family. I've got a wife and grandkids. Years ago I never thought the day would come when any of that would matter. But I guess when you get older some things change," he said, looking wistful.

"Where's your family?" Rosa asked.

"Chicago. Working in New York, Philly, or D.C., maybe, is about as far as I can stand to be away from my family," he said with a glimmer in his eyes.

"Yes, I can understand," she replied, smiling.

"Okay, lovely lady," the seasoned musician said. You've got my card. Call me. I'll be working in New York a few months, even after I leave The Blue Phoenix. Let me know when you're free for lunch or dinner. We'll talk about your career."

"All right," she said, as she watched him disappear backstage to finish taking his break with the other musicians. She slipped his card down the front of her dress and tucked it in her bra. *I'll keep his card, but I doubt that I'll contact him. I already have an agent. And I don't need a manager.*

Rosa spoke to a few more patrons in the club before slipping back stage to her dressing room. One of the club's staff persons played recorded music while Rosa and the band were on their break.

That night, Rosa and the band performed three more sets. Between those sets, the handsome middle-aged trumpet player did not chat with Rosa. He stayed with the other band members. After the final set, most of the band said good-night to Rosa. The trumpet player exited the club without a parting word to anyone. Rosa thought that was a little odd. She kept his card anyway.

The next week when Rosa called home to talk with her parents and let them know how life was going for her in New York, her father was not in, so Rosa talked only with her mother.

"Hi Mama, I just called to let you and Papa know I'm doing all right here in the big city."

"Good, good," Nora replied. "You're taking care of your health, aren't you? You know how easy it is for you to catch a cold."

"Yes, Mama, I'm doing fine. I'm eating right and staying warm. Haven't had any colds since I've been here."

"Good. How's everything at The Blue Phoenix going?"

"Great. I'm drawing good crowds. The owner likes my style. The band is great. What can I say? Life is good."

"I'm so glad. Your father will be sorry he missed your call, but I'll tell him you're doing well up there."

"Okay, Mama. I don't want to talk up a big phone bill, so I won't keep you."

"All right, dear," Nora said.

"Oh! There's one other thing I want to tell you, before I let you go. One night at the club, I met this old musician, and he went on and on giving me advice. He said I should put Paris in my plans, 'cause it would do a lot for my career after I return to the States."

"He's probably right about that, Rosa."

"The way he explained it, I believed him. And, oh yeah, he said he played in Paris over twenty years ago. It was probably before I was born. I wondered if you and Papa might have seen him play when you were Paris."

"We went to a fair amount of jazz clubs that year. We did see a lot of different musicians play. What's his name?"

"Vernon Cooper. You ever see him play?"

Nora's face turned so pale that she looked like she was going to faint. Her legs nearly buckled. Grabbing the back of an armchair nearby was the only thing that kept her from falling to the floor in astonishment.

"Mama, are you still there?"

"...Uh....Uh, yes dear," Nora stammered. "I'm here." She cleared her throat. I-uh, I thought I heard someone at the door. I was trying to listen to be sure, that's all. There's no one there, after all."

"Well, I just wanted to catch you up on what was happening, and let you know I'm okay. Give Papa my love. Tell Willie and Dot I say hello, okay? Oh, yeah, give my love to Grandpa, too."

"I will, honey. Take care of yourself."

"Okay, Mama, I will. I Love you."

"I love you too, baby. Bye-bye now," Nora said, trying to sound as cheerful as possible.

Nora hung up the phone. She swayed while inching her way to the front of the armchair. She sat down and remained still, staring out the window, glassy eyed, as if she might be thinking back in time to the day Rosa was born and how fearful she was on that day, fearful that it might become obvious that Rosa was Vernon Cooper's child.

When Rosa was a new infant, Douglas noticed her ears were much darker brown than the rest of her body. He had heard the women of his mother's family say that the color of a new baby's ears indicated what the baby's overall coloring would ultimately become. So Douglas did have questions for Nora, especially when it became apparent that baby Rosa's coloring was much darker than Nora's honey yellow complexion. The baby's skin was also darker than his own pecan brown color. Although he was not direct in expressing his doubt about the paternity, his thoughts about it showed in his insinuating comments and in his facial expressions. However, Nora did her best to make Douglas feel guilty about even thinking that way.

Evidently Douglas did not really want to doubt that the child was his; for soon he ceased making insinuating comments and looking strangely at tiny Rosa. He began letting his love of the baby have free reign.

Nora's saving grace was that Rosa's facial features: the tapering of her nose, the setting of her eyes, the shape of her ears, turned out to be like Nora's. And Rosa's coloring, although dark brown, turned out to be like some of her relatives on Douglas's side of the family. Rosa's build, as well, turned out to be like that of Douglas's paternal aunts.

Nora would take to her grave her more than twenty year-old secret. The secret resulted from the year she spent in Paris studying art. In the spring of 1925, she met Douglas and a few other people with whom she became fast friends.

Nora Johnson and Douglas Stills were just friends for most of Nora's time in Paris. Douglas had already been living in Paris and working as a hotel doorman when Nora arrived there. After becoming fast friends, they began eating out together and going to nightclubs to dance and enjoy jazz music. One night they went to a club where Vernon Cooper arrived late, carrying his horn. He was invited on stage to play his trumpet along with the band. After he played, Douglas, who already knew Vernon casually, introduced him to Nora and other friends at their table. Nora's attraction to Vernon was immediate and electric. Innately she knew handsome Vernon Cooper, with his brilliant white smile and demeanor of a player of women would not be right for her, but she was compelled to have an affair with him anyway.

Vernon and Nora had a wonderfully romantic, carefree affair in Paris for months. But when Vernon was ready to end the affair, Nora was not, and she had a nervous breakdown as a result of his ultimately lying to her, verbally abusing her, humiliating her, and ignoring her.

Douglas was a loyal friend to Nora throughout her healing process. After she was healed, Nora was totally finished with Vernon. She had no feelings left for him at all.

She ultimately grew to love Douglas and married him a couple of months before they were to return to the United States together. Douglas gave up his Paris apartment and he and Nora lived in her apartment while waiting for the month of May 1926, their time to board a ship back to the States.

One day, a few weeks before Nora and Douglas were to sail for America, Vernon came to their apartment. Nora was there alone. Vernon was drunk and forceful and he raped her. The rape resulted in Nora being pregnant with Vernon's child. Nora was angry, saddened, and fearful. Her fear is what held her together. She feared that if Douglas found out about the rape, he would be angry and deeply hurt, and that hence their marriage would be in jeopardy. She could not risk that happening. So she never told Douglas about the rape. On the ship back to the States, Nora informed Douglas that she was pregnant, letting him believe the baby was his child.

Several months after Nora and Douglas arrived in the States and began living in Washington, D.C., in Nora's parents' home, the baby was born. It was February 1927, and they named the baby Rosa Johnson Stills. Douglas loved baby Rosa. And Nora, for the sake of her marriage and her family's happiness, vowed never to reveal to her husband or anyone else that Rosa was not Douglas's biological child.

The telephone interrupted Nora's thoughts. She rose and answered it. This time Douglas was at the other end of the line. She told him Rosa had called and said she was doing well in New York, and that her job at The Blue Phoenix was secure.

Douglas was excited to hear the news. He had always been Rosa's biggest fan.

Nora went on to talk to Douglas about home things, and while doing so, she sounded like a person whose attention was divided.

CHAPTER 31

▼

New York
November 1950

Rosa missed a couple of menstrual periods and experienced intermittent nausea. She sought the advice of a doctor in New York. He questioned her, then examined her and discovered she was pregnant. Her heart sank; because she had not planned to become a mother. And panic overwhelmed her, for she did not know whether it was Parker's baby or Alan's child. She left the doctor's exam room feeling depressed, and in the outer office, mechanically scheduled her next appointment. Managing a weak smile, Rosa thanked the efficient receptionist, and tried to look happy like a woman who wanted to receive that kind of news. But even as she walked down the street heading towards her neighborhood, she knew she would not keep the baby. After all, she was not ready to be a mother. She had a career to further. Parker was certainly not ready for fatherhood. Neither was Alan.

Even as Rosa tossed those thoughts around in her head, she was planning to locate a doctor who would abort the pregnancy. But not before she had a little fun with Parker and Alan. She broke the news first to Parker.

He laughed and said, "You must be kidding."

She didn't crack a smile.

He then became serious. "What in the hell were you thinking? Evidently you're not as smart as I thought you were," he said, his voice rising with each word.

"Are you crazy?" Rosa asked. "Baby, I'm twice as smart as you thought I was, and then some. I'm going to take care of this baby myself. But if I ever need help, I know a man who would be glad to help me raise it."

"Who?" Parker demanded. "Ain't no body gon' be with you but me, you understand?"

"I understand I've got a career and my own life to live, whether it includes you or not!"

"Watch your mouth little girl. I don't want to have to put you in your place with that baby in your belly. But if you push me too far, I'll do just that."

"And you will surely go to jail!" Rosa shouted, clutching her purse in which she knew she had a knife, "because I *will* press charges against you if you raise a hand to hurt me. And I know plenty of lawyers who'll be glad to help send you up the river."

"Just watch it," Parker said. I'll help you take care o' things. Like you said, you gotta career. So you better get rid of it before too much time passes."

"Leave me alone, Parker. Just get out of here, please. I need some rest. I need to think."

"What's there to think about? Just let me know when you want to have it done, and I'll set things up with the right doctor. It won't be any back alley stuff. You got too much class for that."

"Oh, yeah? You realize that, huh?"

"O' course I realize it. Why you think I want to hold onto you like I do? You all I got to make me look good and classy."

"Well treat me like I deserve it. Right now I need you to leave me alone, so I can get some rest. I've got to go to the club tonight, and I want to look fresh and feel rested when I get there."

He pulled her to him in a warm embrace, kissed her hair, and then spoke low volume into her ear, "All right, baby. You go on and rest. I always want you to look your best for your audience, but mostly for me." He slowly released her, and then left her apartment.

CHAPTER 32

▼

Washington, D.C.

Alan returned from his New York business trip on a Thursday afternoon, and went straight to his LeDroit Park home. Iris spotted him from a lace-curtained window framed by tan drapes, before he entered their Victorian style house.

"Hi," he said upon entering the house.

"Well, hello. You're back," she said with ice in her tone, as she dusted lamp tables.

He kissed her dutifully on her cheek, and then dropped his brief case in the living room, on the shiny hard wood floor near their brown sofa and mahogany coffee table. He then climbed the stairs to the bedroom and pulled off his navy blue suit, white shirt, and print tie, flung them on the bed, and changed into a comfortable sweater the color of pomegranite and a pair of black pants. He trotted back downstairs, retired to the living room sofa and read a few magazines and daily papers to catch up on the news.

Later while tidying their bedroom, Iris haphazardly pulled his suit and shirt from the bed. A pack of matches with the club name where she'd heard Rosa worked fell from his coat pocket, along with his handkerchief; which had lipstick smudges on it. Iris didn't say anything to him about her findings.

The next morning, however, she laid his coat on the bed and laid the packet of matches and lipstick-smudged handkerchief on top of his coat; so that Alan would know she knew he had seen Rosa while he was in New York.

When Alan discovered what Iris had done, he said nothing to her about it. Neither did she confront him. But each was aware the other knew what was going on. Iris said good morning to him in a chilly voice. She told him she was going to her friend Julia Cooke's house for brunch and therefore would not be having breakfast with him. He shrugged it off, taking it in stride as part of the distant relationship their marriage had become. He proceeded to make himself a breakfast of coffee and rolls with butter and jam.

Iris, wearing a charcoal skirt and sweater under a light gray wool coat walked towards the front door, while Alan was in the kitchen eating his breakfast and reading one of several newspapers on the table. She left the house, slid into her white Cadillac, and drove away.

She drove a few blocks to Julia's three-story brownstone house. Julia's Buick was parked in front of the house. Iris noticed that Julia's husband Ted's Chrysler was not behind the Buick, indicating he was either at work or out of town; so she parked in his usual space.

When Julia opened her front door and saw Iris, her eyes widened in surprise. But she quickly welcomed her. "Hey, girl, come on in," she said, pulling her peach-colored robe over her chest as chilly air blew into the house while Iris was stepping inside. "To what do I owe the pleasure of this visit?" she asked.

"Alan's acting up again. Or should I say, he's being his usual self. Nothing's changed, Julia. I just need to talk."

"This calls for coffee and sustenance, Julia said. "Come to the kitchen with me. We'll sit you at the table while I make coffee. We can talk as long as you want. Ted is at Freedmen's Hospital all day. So we won't have any interruptions."

"That's good. Thanks, Julia,"

"We women have to support each other, you know?"

"You know I know," Iris replied.

As Julia prepared coffee, they continued talking, but not yet about the real subject: Alan.

As they talked, Iris gazed out the kitchen window onto the narrow, grassy backyard. The gray sky matched her mood.

When the coffee was ready, Julia pulled two cups from the cupboard, poured some of the hot brew into two cups and set them on the table. She placed a few blueberry muffins on one small tray and arranged cantaloupe cubes, orange slices, and grapes on another. Finally, she placed a small platter of turkey, ham, and cheese slices in the center of the table. Over coffee and their food, Iris confided her suspicions and concerns to Julia.

Listening patiently until Iris expressed all her concerns, Julia sat her coffee cup down and finally spoke.

"You know, Iris," she began, "When you have as much as you and Alan have in terms of money, credentials, connections and status, its best for you to be calm and stay with him."

"I'm trying to do that, Julia, as difficult as it sometimes is."

"I know, I know," Julia said. "I know it's hard. But women like us are smart to keep what we have. Our husbands will one day cool down, and lose their doggish natures. Their mistresses will then be the losers—not you, not me. Always, always remember that, okay, honey?"

"Yes, yes, of course you're right," Iris said.

"I know. I've seen proof of it in my parents' marriage and in countless other marriages run by what I call the smartest of the smart wives," Julia said, with a slow grin crossing her freckled, mushroom-colored face.

Iris hugged her and she responded, holding onto the sisterly embrace for a long moment.

With Iris consoled, the old friends moved on to other subjects and enjoyed their visit.

CHAPTER 33

▼

New York City

Alan went to New York a week later and phoned Rosa when he arrived. She met him in his hotel room, so as not to take a chance on Parker discovering them together at her apartment.

She broke the news of her pregnancy to Alan. Contrary to what she expected, he smiled and said they could make a way to take care of the baby. "Even when you're away I can help support our child. We can hire a governess to be with him or her when you have to perform here in New York, and even when you have a gig away from the city. And I can be in the child's life often. I'll make sure I have a lot of reasons to come to New York. We can be a family, you know?"

"I know what? Are you saying you would not divorce Iris? You would not marry me and live with me and our child?"

"Rosa, you know I can't do that," he said low volume, expressing fatigue at having had to tell her that same thing so many times."

"Well, it's just as well", she retorted. "At least as far as our *dream* family is concerned. You see, Alan, there won't really *be* a baby," she added, watching his face closely for a reaction.

"Wait a minute, Rosa. What are you talking about? What are you saying?"

"I'm *saying* I took care of it." She said coldly. "The baby, I mean. There isn't going to be one," she added, twisting the knife in his psyche.

Stunned, Alan looked remorseful and grief-stricken. His face flushed, and then turned pale. Looking down, he closed his eyes a moment and cleared his throat, as if trying to control himself, to keep from crying. Then, turning away from her, he walked slowly to an armchair and sat down. He leaned over, and with his elbows touching his thighs; he covered his face with his hands, and let out a long, heavy sigh. Then, with his hands holding the sides of his face, he said, "I never thought you'd lie to me like that, Rosa."

She felt sorry for him for only a moment. What surprised her was that she was not instantly turned off by his behavior. For some sick reason, she concluded, she loved him even more in that moment. But when that moment passed, she felt the need to lash out at him.

"Yeah, well I never thought you'd be lying to me this long either."

"What do you mean," he answered, sullen.

"You know very well what I mean. You've been living a lie. Pretending we have a real life together when you're here, then going back and living your other lie with Iris; who knows, by the way, that you don't really love her. She knows you love me, but she doesn't have the sense to let you go, and you don't have the guts to leave her. We all lie to each other. So don't you *dare* tell me you never thought I'd lie to you! You've been lying to yourself, Iris and me for months, even years!" She yelled at him. "And you dared to think I would bring a child into this world and raise it to live a lie along with the rest of us? Surely you have lost your mind!"

"Rosa, look—"

—"Look, nothing!" Rosa shouted. "YOU look. You talk about the wrongness of me killing our baby. Let me just tell you something. Right now the sight of you disgusts me. I'm sick of you. Sick of seeing you in secret…of helping you live your lies…helping you have it all your way: a loveless, money marriage, along with a mistress who totally satisfies you on the side. I'm the one on the losing end here, not you. You're right about one thing, though. I shouldn't have killed the baby. I should have killed YOU," she shouted with rage, as she grabbed her coat and headed towards the door. With her hand on the doorknob, she said, "I'm leaving and I won't be back. Don't try to see me before you leave town. And don't expect to see me at Thanksgiving or Christmas. I'm not going home for either holiday, and I don't want you coming here. I'm through with you, Alan! You hear me? I'm through!" She opened the door, stormed out of the room, and stomped down the hall towards the building's exit.

CHAPTER 34

▼

New York
January 1951

On a cold, bleak Tuesday morning, Alan returned to New York "on business," and went straight to Rosa's apartment. They were so hungry for each other that Rosa knew he would not leave her at the end of the week, as he told her he would. She showed him no signs of the anger and hostility she had displayed during their encounter a couple of months ago. She had sex with him during his January trip to New York; because she wanted the quality of lovemaking she felt only he could provide. After a couple of torrid lovemaking sessions, Rosa told Alan to book a hotel room for the rest of his stay. When he asked why, she said, "It'll make the rest of our time together even more exciting for me. I'm always in my apartment. Going to a hotel with you will change things up a bit, that's all." Alan did not argue the point.

However, Rosa's real reason for wanting a hotel room was that she did not want to take a chance on Parker coming to her place and discovering Alan there. She had heard stories about Parker and his gangster side and learned he was capable of committing major harm, even murder, to people he wanted out of his way. The rumors plus Parker's own threats to kill any man he caught her with made her take his dangerous side seriously.

As far as she and Alan were concerned, she was still angry with him and intended to act out that anger. But she would wait until he finished satisfying her sexual needs that had been pent up for the last couple of months. She would then feel strong enough to tell him what was on her mind and let him go.

Yes, she would confront Alan with her anger later, just before he was ready to return to D.C. After all the years of sharing him with Iris, Rosa was tired. And she was tired of being tired of being the other woman. Yet she knew she still loved him. She felt torn by her dual feelings: wanting to put him permanently out of her life, yet wanting to keep him but all to herself. Lately, she had become crazed by the thought of what the latter choice meant: If she could not have him all to herself; then no one else was going to have him either.

*   *   *   *

Alan informed Rosa on Wednesday evening that he wouldn't be going back to D.C. on the weekend after all. Of course Rosa knew this on the day he arrived in New York. She knew he was going to want to be with her as long as he could arrange it. When Alan informed Iris of his updated plans on Wednesday as well, Iris gave him a hard way to go. He reacted by hanging up the phone while she was in the middle of shouting insults into the phone.

On Friday night while Rosa was at The Blue Phoenix, Alan was in his hotel room, which Rosa had asked him to secure. Alan did not know her reason had to do with her fear of a possessive lover and that she wanted to lessen the chances of that person learning she had a relationship with Alan.

After using the hotel room desk to work a while on some briefs for cases he was handling, Alan stood and stretched. He then put the papers he had worked on inside a folder on the desk and placed the ink pens he had used back in the tray of pens, pencils, paper clips and other items the hotel management must have thought their business guests could use.

Alan showered and dressed, preparing himself to go to The Blue Phoenix around eleven o'clock and catch Rosa's later sets. The two had agreed to come to the hotel room after her last set.

*   *   *   *

At the club, Rosa, having generously allowed a local talent to do a complete set, told the manager, she was going home and should be back in about forty minutes. If she didn't make it back in forty minutes, Rosa mused, the local talent would be a lucky singer that night. Rosa had decided to surprise Alan by going to the hotel room early. She wanted finally to tell him about Parker and let Alan know she believed Parker might have somehow found out about their relationship.

Meanwhile, Parker had told one of his gangster friends he was going to get rid of the man who was trying to take Rosa from him.

PART III

▼

CHAPTER 35

▼

Friday night
Alan's Hotel Room

While waiting until it was time for him to go and see Rosa perform her late night sets, Alan settled back in an arm chair with his legs outstretched. With one hand under his chin, he seemed to be in a pensive mood. Perhaps he was thinking about the long distance talk he had had with Iris two days ago. He had told her he was not coming home this weekend after all.

"Why *aren't* you coming home this weekend?" Iris had asked evenly. "It never took you longer than a week to complete your business in New York before."

"A couple of clients couldn't meet with me on the day and time they originally scheduled," Alan replied. "We rescheduled for early next week. So rather than come home today or tomorrow and have to come right back to New York next week, I decided to just stay here until next week, meet with them, and then come home. It's not a big deal, Iris. I should be back in D.C. by next Wednesday. No later than Thursday."

Iris said, "You know, Alan...I'm getting just a little bit tired. Correction. I am truly fed up with all these trips you're taking to New York. I know they're not all for business. Do you think I'm *stupid* or something?" She said the words stupid or something with exasperation and in a high soprano tone.

"Taking the offensive is out of character for you isn't it, Iris? You've always been the suffer-in-silence type," he said with a smirk in his tone. "Or maybe I've really never known you all these years."

"You don't know me as well as you *think* you know me," she said, her voice filled with anger and sarcasm."

"Calm down, Iris. You need to stop being insecure."

"Insecure! Damn it, Alan. Please don't insult my intelligence. All of Washington knows you've been running around on the sly, sleeping with that whore, Rosa Stills, for years."

"Watch your mouth, Iris."

"I've been watching my mouth for too long," she said, her voice rising to a fever pitch. "I'm serving you notice right now, Alan Covington! If you don't break up with that woman, I will not only divorce you. I will see that you lose your job and never get a position with another law firm in this city or any other city for that matter!"

Alan said nothing for a moment. It was as if he deliberately took the moment to gather his wits and steel his reserve, while Iris was breathing heavy uncontrolled anger into the phone.

He finally spoke, in an even commanding voice. "Just keep this in mind: If you follow through with any one of those threats, be ready to breathe your last breath; because I will surely kill you, no matter what it costs me." He had never displayed that sort of venomous, controlled anger and steely emotion before.

Stunned, Iris was silent.

"I'll see you next week—Maybe!" Alan said coldly and then slammed down the phone.

CHAPTER 36

▼

Friday Night

After leaving it to a local singer to do her 11:00 p.m. set, at The Blue Phoenix, Rosa stopped by her own apartment. She wanted to freshen up before going to Alan's hotel room. As she turned the key in her door, she heard heavy footfalls hurrying up the steps towards her second floor apartment. She turned the door-knob, and just before pushing it to let herself inside, she turned to see who was behind her. Fearful surprise filled her eyes when she saw Parker's big frame loom-ing over her.

Parker smiled at her in a sinister way. He seemed pleased with himself for catching up with her, and possibly catching her in the wrong. Before she could say a word, he pushed the door open and stepped inside before she could enter. "Why don't you come on in?" he said, as he took off his jacket and casually laid it across a chair near her desk; which was piled with sheet music, writing tools, and miscellaneous items.

Not wanting to show her fear, Rosa shouted at him with false bravado. "What are you doing here, Parker? You can't stay. I'm only going to be here a minute myself. I've got someplace to go before I go back to The Blue Phoenix to do my last couple of sets."

"Yeah, I bet you do have someplace you *want* to go. But baby, you ain't goin' there tonight." He said in a threatening tone. "In fact, you ain't ever goin' back there again!" He said, in a raised voice, as he grabbed her arm.

"Get out of my way, Parker," Rosa shouted, pulling her arm away. "And get out of my place! You're not anything but a gangster, a criminal, using that restau-rant as a front for your number running and pimping and who knows what all. I don't want to be around you and your low-life friends anymore," she shouted. "Now get out!"

CHAPTER 37

▼

He'd threatened her before but never hit her. This night was different. Outraged by her insults and actions, he backhanded her face, rocking and hurling her to the floor. She lay still, appearing unconscious. Her eyes ballooned. Tears rushed down her cheeks, evidencing her pain. The fusion of his citrus cologne and natural musk assaulted her nostrils. In a moment, a few of her fingers flexed. Her arms and legs moved a little. It was apparent she was regaining her senses and strength and would momentarily rise from the carpet.

Diving to the floor, he over-reached for her and merely grazed one of her arms. She winced. Quickly realizing again what was happening, she cried out and scrambled away from him, across the carpet to the desk. Straining her arm, she grabbed a leg of the leather armchair at the desk and pulled her body up high enough to let her free hand reach for something. Her fingers discerned a tray filled with pencils, pens, and possibly a letter opener. She then felt and latched onto what she knew would serve her best. Wrapping her fingers around the scissors, she yanked them from the desk a split second before he grabbed her foot and clutched her ankle.

With greater control of her, he gripped the back of her leg, between the knee and thigh. She clung to the sturdy chair leg with one hand and to the scissors with the other. Then, stabbing backwards blindly and fiercely, she lacerated something.

He jerked away from her, cursing as he saw rich red blood from his hand spurting everywhere.

Shoeless and with her sweater and torn skirt splattered with his blood, she pulled herself up with the help of the desk leg. Still gripping the scissors, she lunged, stabbing him in the face, neck, anywhere and everywhere until he lost his ability to fight back or even keep his eyes open. Holding his head he fell to his knees, then slumped to the floor and lay still, breathing laboriously.

She looked down at his motionless bleeding flesh, then quickly bent down and retrieved her purse from the floor near his body. Purse in one hand, she gently touched her bruised, aching face with the other. She moved towards a chest of drawers with a large mirror above it, and inspected the damage he had done to the side of her face. Then, with a handkerchief from her purse she walked around the room and wiped off seemingly every surface her hands had touched.

Afterwards, she retrieved the bloody scissors from the floor, took them to the bathroom, and washed and dried them with a towel. Giving the instrument that saved her life a final once-over from tip to handles, she held the scissors within her handkerchief and returned them to the desk tray.

She found her shoes and slipped them back on her feet. She then pulled his jacket from the chair it lay across and slid her arms into its sleeves. It hung on her like a coat and hid her torn, blood-stained clothing well. Pulling the coat-like jacket around herself, she opened the door and left, found an exit at the rear of the building, and slipped into the wintry night.

CHAPTER 38

▼

When the police showed up at Rosa's apartment the next day, she was nervous and appeared bewildered. The detectives questioned her as to her whereabouts the previous evening between 11:00pm and midnight. Rosa told them she had gotten a local singer to perform her 11:00 set at The Blue Phoenix. She left the club shortly before 11:00, intending to surprise her friend by showing up at his hotel room. But at the last minute she changed her mind and went to her apartment instead. She decided to meet her friend later, outside the club after her last set, as he was expecting her to do.

"Is there anyone who can corroborate your alibi?" one of the detectives asked.

"The manager at The Blue Phoenix and others at the club can vouch for when I left the club and when I got back."

"Who can verify that you were at home during your break from the Club?"

"Why? Why are you asking me these questions?" Rosa asked with apprehension and defensiveness in her voice.

The detective then informed Rosa that Alan Covington was found murdered in his hotel room.

She stared at the police in stunned disbelief.

While Rosa was trying to fathom the horrible news, there was a knock at the door, but Rosa didn't hear it. She became feverish and nauseous. Her knees and legs were wobbly and no longer wanted to support her. She raised her hand to her forehead, her eyes closed involuntarily, and her body spiraled to the floor. As one of the detectives bent to help her, the other officer opened the door for the mysterious visitor.

When Rosa regained consciousness, she was lying on the sofa, surrounded by two detectives and the visitor. One of her new friends, Gwendolyn Newsome, who lived in Harlem, had simply been in Rosa's neighborhood and stopped by unannounced.

Now by her side, Gwen gave Rosa some water, then a cup of hot tea, which she sipped while listening to the detectives and answering more of their questions.

She did not know who committed the murder, but she mentioned Parker as a possible suspect.

"Are you saying you did or did not go to Mr. Covington's hotel room?"

"I did not go," Rosa said. "I mean, I was going to go, like I said. But then, when I stopped by my apartment first, to freshen up, Parker was at my apartment. He forced his way inside my place. He told me he knew about Alan, and he was going to get him. Somehow he found out about Alan and where Alan was staying. Parker left my place, and he gave me the distinct impression he was going to Alan's hotel. That's why I ended up not going to Alan's hotel room. I wouldn't have made it there before Parker. I tried calling the hotel, to warn Alan, but for some reason my call didn't go through. At that point, I was in no shape to go back to work, and I didn't want to spend the night pacing around my apartment. So I had a drink to try to relax a little. The one drink didn't work, so I had a couple more. It might have been three more, I stopped counting. Anyway, I laid my tired body down. Or maybe I fell onto the bed. I don't know, but I didn't wake up until this morning, when I heard your knock on the door."

Rosa explained how jealous and possessive Parker was, and how he had said if he ever found out she was seeing another man, he would kill the man.

After learning his address from Rosa, the police arrested Parker. They picked up another suspect, Milton Thurman—an average looking, mediocre New York attorney that Rosa named as one of Alan's enemies. Thurman had sprung from a poor family and had struggled through law school, struggled to attain big cases, and struggled to win the attention and affection of women.

Thurman hated Alan; it was rumored; because everything came easy for Alan. Women came easy. Making it through law school, the bar exam; marrying into the right family; and making it into one of the most respected Colored law firms in D.C. and on the East Coast—all seemed easy for Alan. Thurman had competed with Alan for a few professional positions and for a few women and lost.

Since he was reportedly one of Alan's enemies, the detectives paid Thurman a visit and escorted him to the police station's criminal division for questioning.

The police questioned Parker and Thurman by turns. Each suspect endured the interrogation with impatience and desired to be done with it as soon as possible. Each man swore he didn't kill Alan Covington. After extensive questioning of both men, the police deduced that although Thurman was a confirmed enemy of Alan's, he did not have a motive to *kill* him. Parker did, they said.

Parker, a racketeer with a police record, had both a predisposition for violence and a motive: his desire to possess Rosa. Parker had somehow found out about Alan and the long-time hold he'd had on Rosa. The police figured Parker probably thought that if he could remove Alan from the picture, then he could have Rosa all to himself.

*   *   *   *

Iris's face turned white when the New York police notified her by telephone that Alan was dead. An intruder killed him in his hotel room approximately two days ago, they informed her. Iris clung to the telephone receiver for a moment without saying a word. Her mother, who was at Iris and Alan's house at the time, observed that Iris's face turned pale and that she was clutching the sofa back edge with her free hand, as if she were trying to keep from falling. Mrs. Haywood pried the phone from Iris's fingers.

"Hello, hello? Who is this?" Mrs. Haywood demanded into the telephone, her light skin turning darker shades of red by the second.

—"I am Gladys Haywood, Iris Haywood Covington's mother.

—"Yes. Of course I'm Alan Covington's mother-in-law! Is something wrong? What's happened? Is my son-in-law all right?

—"What?" Mrs. Haywood asked, in shock as her free hand flew to her chest. "There must be some mistake!

—"Wait a minute, wait a minute! Are you absolutely sure it's Alan Covington, my son-in-law. Attorney Alan Covington of Washington, D.C.

—"Oh, my god. Oh, my goodness. Oh…Oh-h-h. Oh, my god. Well, what, how did it happen? Who—

—"All right. All right, of course, Sir. You say Alan's body has been positively identified already?" Mrs. Haywood asked.

—Okay. Okay. And you say you've already spoken with his parents, Mr. and Mrs. Covington?"

—"They're going to arrange to have the body transported back here to D.C.? All right, then. If they've already told you that, then my daughter won't have to worry about taking care of that. Okay. All right, I'll talk with the Covingtons this evening. Please keep me informed of the investigation, won't you, Detective Roy? I am my daughter's representative. She's in no condition to speak with anybody outside the family. Yes. You can reach me here. I'll be staying with my daughter until everything is taken care of and the investigation is complete.

—"Yes, Sir. Yes. Yes. All right. Goodbye," Mrs. Haywood said, then placed the receiver on its hook. With both hands, she pulled back her mixed brown and gray hair, moved her tongue over her lips, seemingly to relieve their dryness; and then holding her arms under her modest bosom, she looked at her daughter.

Iris, having sunk into a brown armchair, looked at her mother, waiting for some answers.

Gladys Haywood, slight of build but strong of demeanor, stared with dark brown eyes at her devastated daughter, confirming the family's worst nightmare.

Iris did not cry. She did not utter a word but just sat there, clutching the chair's arms with her hands, staring blankly into space.

After Alan's body was transported back to D.C., Iris managed, with her mother's and Mrs. Covington's help, to make arrangements for Alan's funeral and burial. After the funeral Iris slumped into mourning. She became reclusive and was seldom seen by the public for many months.

CHAPTER 39

▼

Late January 1951

Rosa traveled to D.C., not to attend Alan's funeral but to be with her family for a while. She did not want to see Alan in a casket or face his family and friends, many of whom knew of her long time illicit relationship with him. Instead, Rosa chose to grieve surrounded by her own family and without talking to them about his death. She did not want to tell them that he took part of her soul to the grave with him.

Rosa wished she had made their last times together happier. She agonized over having aborted their child. If she had kept it, she would still have something of Alan. And she would not care what people might have said about her being an unwed mother, or what they might have whispered if the baby had looked just like Alan.

Rosa kept her photos of Alan close, always carrying one in her purse or luggage. She began taking long walks in her neighborhood to be alone with her memories of him. Once, she drove her father's car to a Colored-owned jewelry store on U Street and bought a golden locket, opened it and placed a tiny photo of Alan inside. She then strung the locket on a gold chain and wore it everyday around her neck, either hanging outside of her dress or tucked in her bosom, close to her heart.

Rosa knew she would never forget Alan, but she wanted the time to come when the pain of losing him would lessen. She longed for the day when she would no longer wrestle with anger and guilt and remorse and sadness. She knew from reading about the stages of grief and from listening to her church's minister that the sting of death and its lingering pain eventually leaves the bereaved. After that happens one remembers only the positive things about the deceased loved one and the happy times one shared with him or her.

Eventually, when Rosa went for walks or attended church, she faced hateful stares from friends of Iris and others who knew she had been Alan's lover for years, even after his marriage to Iris. And on occasion, when the haters said nice-nasty remarks to her, she returned their insulting comments with words as cutting as theirs were to her.

*   *   *   *

Meanwhile, in the LeDroit Park area of D.C., Iris was under her doctor's care. He prescribed medication for her deep depression and pills to help her sleep. And still, according to her family and visiting friends, she was despondent every day. After a few months passed with no difference in her condition, the doctor changed Iris's medication.

Her parents considered taking her to visit family in Atlanta and letting her stay with them for a while. They finally decided a complete change of scenery should help Iris move forward in her recovery.

However, as it turned out, Iris had other plans. One night, she consumed a handful of sleeping pills, forcing them down with a glass of water. She then lay on her bed, pulled a volume of poems from her nightstand and opened it to a poem by William Cullen Bryant, titled *Thanatopsis*. Her eyes moved to the poem's last verse; which she read slowly to herself, lingering on the final lines:

> *...sustained and soothed*
> *By an unfaltering trust, approach thy grave*
> *Like one who wraps the drapery of his couch*
> *About him, and lies down to pleasant dreams.*

Iris closed her eyes and never opened them again.

The note Iris left for her parents told them she was the one who killed Alan. She had traveled to New York and killed him, she added, because she could no longer stand the thought of him with Rosa or any other woman. She ended the note with, "And now I am going to join Alan. We will be together, peacefully...forever." The note was signed, "Your loving daughter, Iris".

Mrs. Haywood gave the suicide note\ murder confession to the D.C. Police Department. They made a copy of it for their files and forwarded the original to the New York City Police.

After the New York police were notified of Alan Covington's real killer, they removed Jackson Parker's name as a suspect in the case.

Parker secured the Johnson, Stills home telephone number in D.C. and dialed it.

"Hello?" Rosa answered.

"For some reason, I didn't think you'd be the one who'd answer the phone," Parker said.

"How did you get this phone number?" Rosa asked in a curt manner.

"Shouldn't the question be, 'How're you doing baby? Or, hi, Parker, I've been missin' you like crazy?" he said.

"I asked you how you got this number!" Rosa demanded.

"I'm gone chalk up your tone of voice and attitude to the fact that your friend got killed. I'm sorry about that. But you got me, baby. That's all you need."

"Look, Parker. I'm not coming back to New York. In fact I'm leaving D.C. soon. I'm moving away…far away. So don't call this number anymore."

"Where you goin?" he demanded, and yet sounding as if he knew he had no control over the situation.

"It doesn't matter where I'm going. I will never see you again. Goodbye, Parker." She quietly hung up the telephone.

C H A P T E R   40

▼

February–May 1951

Fortunately Rosa's contract with The Blue Phoenix had ended shortly after Alan's funeral, allowing her to spend a few months with her family and give considerable thought to what she was going to do next. She knew she wanted to live somewhere other than D.C. and New York, the cities in which sights and sounds triggered painfully nostalgic memories of Alan. She desired to go to a far away place where it would be easier for her to start a new life. Her mind flashed back to her conversation with Vernon Cooper who had advised her that performing for a time in Paris would help her career. Realizing, then, that living and working in Paris would serve two important needs, Rosa decided to go there.

Rosa asked a few of her sorority sisters and New York friends who had lived in Paris to give her contact information for a couple of their friends in Paris and also some suggestions for safe places to live there. Michael Goldberg, Rosa's friend and former agent, agreed to use his contacts to help her land a singing job in Paris.

Rosa informed her mother and father about her decision and that she would be going as soon as her old agent lined up a job for her in Paris.

Douglas seemed concerned that Rosa was making her move too soon after her loss. He told her he did not know if she was ready to handle being that far away from family.

Nora reminded Douglas that Paris had turned out to be good for the two of them, hadn't it? And the big change would help Rosa move on with her life. In the final analysis, Rosa's parents agreed she was strong and would be all right. Hadn't she made a living for herself in New York? That success had shown she was definitely not faint hearted or weak minded, they concurred.

Nora promised Rosa she would write to her and Douglas's old Paris friends, Henri and Lenore Monnier and let them know Rosa would be in Paris. She was also going to give Rosa their address and phone number.

Grandpa William was all for seeing Rosa follow her mind and her heart, just as he had been in support of Nora, when she was young.

Willie encouraged Rosa to follow her own mind. He wished her the best in Paris. Willie was going to his meetings designed to help struggling alcoholics overcome their addiction, and he had managed to win back his woman and pull his life together.

Dot was so caught up in her own life that she had little to say about Rosa moving to Paris except, "Have fun, big sister. Write me if you get a chance. If you don't, just send me your regards through Mama and Papa. I know you'll keep in touch with them. See you later, girl. I'm on my way out to meet some very important people."

Rosa knew Willie would always be the same: No matter what was going on with him, he would take time out to encourage her and wish her happiness. She also knew that Dot would remain the same: self absorbed and self-serving.

With her parents', Grandpa William's, and Willie's blessings, Rosa felt bolstered. For although she knew no one could stop her from relocating to Paris, it was still important, she felt, to have family support.

CHAPTER 41

▼

Paris, France
June 1951

Michael Goldberg secured a contract for Rosa at Chez Jolene, a popular night-club in Montparnasse, on the Left Bank. Through his business associates, he arranged a furnished apartment for her in the same Paris neighborhood.

Rosa traveled for fifteen hours on an Air France jet from the United States to Paris. Her flight landed at Paris's Orly Airport, and she took a taxi to her apartment in Montparnasse. After paying her fare and seeing the driver pull away, she found her unit inside the apartment building, dropped her luggage on the floor, wandered from the living room into the bedroom, and fell across the bed. She slept until late afternoon.

When she woke up, she found the bathroom and discovered a set of brand new white towels and washcloths lying on a small table next to the basin for her use. *Michael or his French contacts seem to have thought of everything*, she mused, a slow smile making its way across her face. *I might have one of the most caring ex-agents in the world.*

After bathing, Rosa dressed in a blue blouse, navy blue skirt, and gray sweater. Wanting to explore her surroundings, she left the apartment for a stroll around the neighborhood. Along the way she saw residents and tourists milling around vegetable and flower markets on the streets. She heard the buzz of lively conversations in English and French filling the air. Rosa noticed bakeries, wine and cheese shops, and outdoor cafés, where some people were enjoying café and croissants and others took delight in salads, and other luncheon fare. She was not hungry yet but made a mental note to stop and buy at least some bread, wine, cheese, and fruit on her way back to the apartment.

Within a couple of days, after Rosa felt somewhat settled in her new place, she went to Chez Jolene for the first time, to meet her new employer. She pulled open the heavy dark green door of the club and stepped inside. What she discovered was an intimate club where, according to Michael Goldberg, renowned jazz musicians and singers came on any given night, after their own gigs at other clubs ended.

Employees were wiping off the bar, sweeping the floor, and straightening tables. In her limited knowledge of the French language and with gestures, Rosa asked a skinny white man with dark curly hair where she might find Monsieur Louis St. Pierre.

"Who wants to know?" a bass voice answered in English from the other end of the small, intimate establishment.

Rosa looked in that direction and saw a handsome man with a commanding presence approaching her. "Rosa Johnson Stills. I'm a jazz singer from Washington, D.C. and New York," she answered. "My agent, Michael Goldberg, negotiated a contract for me to sing here. Are you Louis St. Pierre?"

"Yes, I am."

She was surprised to see he was Colored. Tall and brown-skinned, he was a little lighter than her father. His black hair was wavy with a touch of gray at each temple and above the sideburns. He was thick bodied and healthy-looking, with a slow smile that captivated Rosa, as he came closer to her.

"I'm very pleased to meet you, Miss Stills," he said in a low rumbling voice, as he extended his hand to her.

"Thank you, Mr. St. Pierre, the feeling is mutual," Rosa responded, shaking his hand.

"Please. Call me Louis."

"All right, Louis. And you can call me Rosa."

"Your good reputation preceded you, Rosa; I look forward to having you display your artistry here.

"Thank you, Louis."

Rosa was attracted to him, but in a way that might encourage a warm, comfortable liaison rather than a hot, unsettling affair. However, she refused to let her wondering thoughts of him linger. She wanted to start and establish a business relationship with him.

"I understand you sometimes accompany yourself on the piano."

"Yes. That's true."

"Good. I just lost a piano player. So if you will accompany yourself, I'll be able to extend your contract when the time comes."

"That sounds good," Rosa said. "Thank you."

"All right. I have a bassist and a drummer who've worked here a long time. I've also got a trumpet player and a saxophonist on my payroll. They'll be here later this afternoon if you want to hang around and meet them. Or you can arrive a little early next Thursday night, when you start, and talk with them then. It's up to you."

"Next Thursday is fine," Rosa replied.

"Okay. Now once you start, you can have whatever you need to work comfortably here. Whatever you require, just ask me or my staff, and we'll see that you get it."

"Thank you, Louis." Rosa pulled something from her pocket. "Here," she said, handing it to him. "I'm on Rue Chateau. My phone number is also on the card. See you next Thursday night." She then turned and walked towards the door.

"Right," Louis replied, looking at the card and then at Rosa's back, skirted hips, and shapely dark brown legs as she reached the door and turned the doorknob. "Next Thursday. Seven o'clock," he said.

"I'll be here," she said, as she opened the thick green door and stepped out of the club, into the afternoon sunlight.

Rosa later learned that Louis was an American, born of Creole parents from New Orleans. He'd been a soldier in World War I. Afterwards, he'd remained in Paris, worked hard and eventually saved enough money to open a restaurant in Montmarte. That venture did well for years. Then, when the Japanese bombed Pearl Harbor, and World War II began, everything changed. France was invaded, the economy changed, businesses were forced to close.

After the War was over, Montmarte was not the same as it had been after World War I and during the interwar period. In the late 1940s, many artists and musicians started favoring the Left Bank as a place to live and work. Entrepreneurs began opening clubs on the Left Bank, and the jazz scene in Paris shifted there. Likewise, Louis opened a new business, Chez Jolene, with a business partner, a white Frenchman. A couple of years later his partner contracted pneumonia and died, leaving Louis St. Pierre as the sole owner of Chez Jolene.

Rosa had taken an immediate liking to Louis. In addition to his robust good looks, he was outgoing. Yet he possessed the reserve necessary for a careful entrepreneur. It was apparent to Rosa that, although he hired her because she was accomplished and talented, he also liked the look of her attractive dark-skinned face and voluptuous shape. She often caught him surveying her figure.

Rosa wanted to hold onto her good memories of Alan Covington, but she needed to shed the heartbreak and the negative publicity surrounding his marriage and death. The distance the ocean put between her and the cities of Alan's life and demise would help. Another thing that would in time help heal Rosa's feelings of loss, she thought, would be a friendship with Louis St. Pierre. But Rosa would not strike up anything with him just yet. She would focus on her work at Chez Jolene. She wanted to be the singer patrons looked forward to seeing and hearing when they came there.

Rosa started her engagement at Chez Jolene on a high note. Her improvisational style of singing, her sometimes sassy, other times scat filled, rich velvet voice captivated her audiences night after night. Jazz lovers kept telling their friends about Rosa and after the word was out, she drew a crowd to the club every night she sang during that first year. The patrons loved her. Their love assured her that her contract at Chez Jolene would be renewed for another two years. In time she became well known all over Paris and was respected as an artist in her adopted city.

CHAPTER 42

▼

1952

In her correspondence with her parents over the months, Rosa talked about her job at Chez Jolene and about how much she liked Paris. "Mama, I see what you and Papa saw in it now," she wrote to Nora.

"The City is beautiful, and the people in Paris are so accepting of Colored artists. I'm starting to understand how living and working in Paris will broaden me and help raise me to another level as an artist."

Also in her letters to Nora and Douglas, Rosa asked for updates on her siblings' activities. She learned that Willie, now at the legal age of twenty-one, was staying sober, keeping a job, and no longer hanging around his old friends. He and Anna, his girl friend of one year, were going to get married soon, and by her pastor. They didn't want a big wedding.

"We love each other. We want to get married and have at least one child and keep making each other happy. That's enough for us," Willie had told Nora and Douglas. They were married by Anna's minister, with no family or guests present.

"She wanted it that way," Willie told his parents. Nora and Douglas had no choice but to accept it.

Rosa learned that Dot, now 19 years old and a junior in college, was an AKA. She was extremely popular on Howard University's campus and off. And she was newly engaged to Hubert Jennings, a resident physician at Freedmen's Hospital. Dr. Jennings, who was tall and light-skinned with black straight hair, hailed from a prominent Philadelphia family.

Dot was fulfilling her destiny, Rosa mused. She was a well connected, soon-to-be doctor's wife, a promising socialite, and a perfect young member of

Washington, D.C.'s Colored elite. Grandma Lilly would have been proud that her favorite grandchild was fulfilling her expectations.

Through her correspondence with Elsie, Rosa learned that her best friend was still happily married.

Elsie was glad to learn Rosa was carving a new life for herself in Paris. "Have you met anyone yet?" Elsie asked in one of her letters. "A man, I mean. Is there any romance in your life? If so, tell me about him. Tell me everything, girl."

Rosa wrote back to Elsie, saying, "There's no romance in my life yet. But there's someone I've got my eye on. Well, I may as well tell you, it's my boss at the club where I'm working. I haven't made a move on him yet, because I'm trying to establish myself as a singer there first. But if he's free when I'm ready to go after him, he *will* be mine. I'll let you know when something happens with us."

Rosa's correspondence from the States also included occasional letters from old New York friends and a note from Molly, a waitress at The Blue Phoenix, who had had eyes for the trumpet player, Vernon Cooper. Molly's most recent letter informed Rosa that she heard Vernon had a stroke. The stroke disfigured his lips and disabled the right side of his body. Therefore he was no longer playing his trumpet. "He's in Chicago fulltime with his family now," Molly wrote.

Rosa was shocked to hear the sad news about Vernon Cooper and felt sorry for him. She would like to have let him know she followed his suggestion, and that their brief encounter had in a way changed her life. But she knew she would never see him or speak with him again.

CHAPTER 43

▼

Rosa finally began to return the romantic interest that Louis St. Pierre showed her. She invited him to her apartment and let him sample her cooking. Although Rosa did not cook every day, she knew her way around the kitchen when she wanted to cook.

Cooking was a creative endeavor for her. Rosa was improvisational with it and never followed a recipe strictly as it was written. She would dress it up or down, incorporate her own personal style, always adding some love into it.

The meal of pot-roast beef, potatoes, carrots, and green beans and a well-chosen red wine boasted Rosa's personal style. Louis had not tasted a meal that good since he was back in the States ten or twelve years ago, he said.

"You mean your woman let you out long enough today to spend this much time with someone else?" she asked.

"What woman?" he said.

"Your woman. Surely you have one somewhere in Paris," she teased.

"There are those who are interested in me. But I haven't taken the time to respond to any of them.

"Oh? Is something wrong with them? Are they all ugly or out of shape, or both?" she probed.

"No. It's just that none of them are the *right* one. I don't believe in sharing my time with people who are not good for me," he said looking directly into her eyes.

"I see," Rosa said, comprehending the meaning of his words and look.

Sometimes Louis would prepare French meals of fish and vegetables with a sauce and white wine for the two of them, at Rosa's apartment. And sometimes he would cook for them at his place above Chez Jolene. They shared their dreams for the future. He wanted to keep her at Chez Jolene as long as she wanted to stay. He also wanted to buy a home somewhere in the French countryside. They became close and began finding time to do things Rosa had not done before; because she had been so focused on establishing herself as a jazz artist at Chez Jolene in particular and in Paris in general.

They strolled around the Left Bank, stopping to buy floral bouquets at flower markets; walked past the world famous high fashion designer houses Givenchy and Christian Dior; and visited the Louvre Museum, which stretched for nearly a half mile. They strolled through the beautiful Tuileries Gardens, and down the Champs Elysees, that world famous promenade of cafés, fashion shops, and restaurants.

Rosa and Louis had lunch at Aux Deux Magots and Café de Flores and other famed cafés that had been haunts of noted writers, visual artists, and patronized by thousands of tourists and natives alike.

Soon Rosa and Louis began spending nights at each other's apartments. After a couple of months, they became known as a couple. Everyone who patronized Chez Jolene knew they were an item. People began asking them when they were going to get married. Rosa hastened to reply, "Maybe never." Then she would look at Louis and say, "We like our relationship the way it is, right baby?"

"Right," he said.

Rosa learned to speak French fluently and began to love Paris with its River Seine and the notable bridges that crossed it. She marveled at the Eiffel Tower and the Notre Dame Cathedral, and enjoyed strolling down the Boulevards Ste. Michel and Ste. Germain. She came to love something about most of the Paris neighborhoods, or *arrondissements*.

Together, Rosa and Louis visited the area on the northern rim of Paris called Montmarte, where the City of Light rises to its highest point. They strolled through the streets of Montmarte, noticing artists painting and tourists exploring the area.

On one of the few nights when Rosa was off from Chez Jolene, she and Louis went to a couple of clubs in Montmarte. Before leaving the area, they climbed the steps of Le Sacre Couer Basilica, its beautiful white dome overlooking the City. Rosa learned that although the Latin Quarter had its magic, Montmarte at night was something special too. It possessed its own magical beauty, and she realized that from that high geographical place, the City truly sparkled.

CHAPTER 44

▼

1953

Rosa loved that Louis had a private self just for her. When they were together, he let go of all the reserve he showed the public. She basked in the undivided attention he gave her, the loving treatment he showered upon her—the flowers and wine, the shopping trips. He often cooked and served her breakfast in bed on Sundays.

Together they took road trips to the South of France. Through all the activities they did together, she could feel his love. And his love drove away all traces of Rosa's dark thoughts, including those concerning the remarks her grandmother used to make to discourage her dreams. Rosa's experiences with Louis eradicated her feelings of rejection; which she used to try to overcome with false bravado and by acting like not having Alan as her own didn't matter to her.

The way Louis treated her showed Rosa that his love was not the short term kind. She was becoming his life. Rosa did not feel the need to marry him to validate their relationship or to hold onto it. For the first time in her life, she was totally secure in a love relationship. As far as a male-female friendship, there was none that could touch hers and Louis's accept her relationship with her father. She knew that although her mother loved her, it was her father who loved her unconditionally.

That secure feeling she felt with Louis, which was akin to the security she felt with her father, complimented the comfortable place she now inhabited in her career.

CHAPTER 45

▼

1953

Thoughts about her parents' eminent visit to Paris excited Rosa. They were coming to see her in the City of Light as a twenty-seventh wedding anniversary gift to themselves. Both in their early fifties, graying, and looking like the grandparents they were—due to Willie's wife having had a baby boy—Nora and Douglas decided they deserved this trip. Besides, contrary to what Nora had thought they might do, they had not revisited Paris since they were married there in 1926.

As far as Rosa was concerned, her parents were returning to Paris at the right time. Her career and her relationship with Louis were both solid. She was thriving professionally and personally. She felt confident, and complete.

Rosa's apartment was small, but she planned to make adjustments so her father and mother could stay with her a few nights. She would sleep in the living room and let them sleep in her room.

In their letters, Douglas and Nora had promised their friends, Henri and Lenore Monnier, that after spending a few nights at Rosa's place, they would spend a few days and nights with them. They planned to visit Henri's mother, Simone Monnier, as well.

Rosa offered to pick them up at Orly airport, but Nora and Douglas insisted on taking a taxi to her apartment. Rosa figured they might have preferred to be by themselves when they viewed the highways leading into the City, as well as the streetscapes of Paris, for the first time in over twenty years. Maybe they wanted to reminisce by themselves as they rode past sites they had experienced when they were young and brand new friends discovering Paris. Rosa decided to honor their wish.

The taxi finally arrived at Rosa's apartment on rue de Chateau. Rosa, having been on the lookout for them, watched from her window as the taxi pulled alongside the beige building in which she lived. A broad smile brightened her face as she saw them step out of the cab.

The taxi driver removed the middle-aged couple's luggage from the cab and set it on the sidewalk. Douglas grabbed the two heavier pieces and Nora took the two smaller bags.

The pale, dark-haired driver then opened his door, slid under the steering wheel, and drove away, leaving the couple, years his senior, with their luggage in hand, facing Rosa's building.

Having raced down the stairs, Rosa pushed open the building door and ran to her parents with a beaming smile and open arms. "Hey-y-y, I'm so glad you're here!" she shouted with extreme excitement in her voice.

Douglas dropped the two suitcases, and Nora let the bags she was holding fall to the pavement, as they reached for Rosa.

Rosa threw one arm around Douglas's neck and the other around Nora's and held on tightly. "Oh, my goodness, I'm so glad to see you two."

"We're glad to see you, too, baby," Douglas said, cheek to cheek with his eldest child. "And it's real special seeing you living in the city where your mother and I met and fell in love."

Nora said to Rosa, "It's good to see you in the flesh and see how good and healthy you look, instead of just seeing you in photographs, you know?"

"Yeah, Mama, I know," Rosa agreed, gradually loosening her hold around their necks. "Hey, well, let's go on up, she said, gesturing and waving one arm towards the building. "I want you to see my little place and get comfortable," she said, grinning and letting both arms fall to her sides.

"Mama, let me help you," Rosa said, lifting Nora's luggage from the ground, and then walking towards the building door. She set one bag down, pulled open the door, and then lifted the bag, saying, "Okay Mama, Papa, follow me upstairs. My apartment is on the second floor."

Once inside her apartment, Nora and Douglas complimented her on its decor. "I like your colors," Nora said, surveying the burnt sienna-colored walls with white baseboards; the sheer off-white curtains, cream-colored lamps, and brown sofa and armchairs.

"Actually, none of this is my doing, Mama. Not even these two framed prints on the walls," Rosa said, pointing to the hanging artwork. "You can tell an amateur did them. They're not professional like your work. In fact they can't even touch your work, Mama," Rosa said.

"Well, I've had a lot of training and I've been working at it a long time, dear."

"That's true," Rosa said. "I'll have you send me a couple of your smaller pieces to hang in here. Your art will really give this place some class, Mama.

"Anyway," Rosa continued, "the place was painted and furnished this way when I moved in. I'm glad I liked it and didn't really have to change it, since I had to start working at Chez Jolene a week after I got here."

"You really were lucky to get such a nice place," Nora said, looking around the room. "I see you've come to like plants a lot, too," Nora commented, peering at the bright green hanging plants and the smaller plants sitting on a table near the window and around the living room.

While mother and daughter chatted, Douglas strolled towards the window, pulled the sheer off-white curtains aside and peered out the window, onto the street. Cars and people trafficked up and down the streets and sidewalks. Residents of the City and visitors went about their business.

"Yes, I love plants now. Signs of life, you know? Some people like cats or dogs. I like plants."

"Plants do help to beautify a room. And in addition to providing oxygen, they give you something to care for and nurture. All of that is good for your health," Nora said.

"Yes, you definitely have to take care of them. They're my children, in a way," Rosa said.

"Okay, Mama and Papa, follow me. Your room is this way." She led them to her bedroom. "Put down your things," she instructed them. "Freshen up and rest if you like. Just make yourselves at home."

"All right, sweetheart," Douglas said. "You've got a real nice place here."

"Thanks, Papa. Now if you want to call your friends, the Monniers, the telephone is in the living room. Feel free to use the phone and anything else you want," she said. She thought a second, and then added, "Why am I telling you this? You're my parents. You can do anything you want. If it weren't for you two, I wouldn't even exist!"

Nora turned red. She may have been reminded of the secret she must carry to her grave: that Douglas was not Rosa's biological father.

"Are you okay, Nora?" Douglas asked. You're all red. What's wrong?"

"Nothing, I'm okay. Forcing a smile she added, "I'm just so excited we're here in Paris. And that we're with our eldest child, the one we haven't seen in so long, that's all."

The three of them hugged, and then Rosa said, "Okay, you too, lighten up. Now get comfortable. We'll talk some more later, and we'll decide where we're going to eat."

*   *   *   *

On her parents' second night in Paris, Rosa had to work at Chez Jolene. She had already walked them past Chez Jolene the evening before, on their way out to eat dinner. They wanted to go inside. But Rosa told them she would take them inside a few evenings later. Then she said, "Actually you're going to spend a couple of nights with Monsieur and Madame. Monnier, right?"

"Right," Douglas replied.

"I think it would be nice if you and Mama would come to the club with them one of those nights. You could have a table near the front. I'll introduce you all to Louis after the first set. It'll be less pressure for me, if we do it that way, okay?"

"Why should there be any pressure?" Nora asked.

"Well, he's much older than I am, that's all."

"How much older?" Nora asked, sounding skeptical.

"He's in his forties…late forties," Rosa replied, stretching her lips east and west and closing one eye tightly, as if she expected disapproval.

"Late forties!" Nora boomed.

"Well, Mama, he seems to be what I need. He just does."

"What do you *mean*, what *you need*?"

"Mama, he's mature. He's intelligent. He knows how to treat people, especially me. He's caring, and I just feel right with him, that's all. He's like Papa, in a way, because he loves me unconditionally. And yet he's different from my father. The important thing is…he lets me be the woman I need to be. I see myself with him for the rest of my life, whether we're married or not."

"What do you mean, whether you're married or not!" Nora asked in a loud tone, demanding clarification or an amended statement.

"Mama…. "Rosa said, exasperated by Nora's reaction.

"Douglas, talk to her," Nora snapped.

Douglas looked at Nora. "Honey, our number one child is a full grown woman, who's experienced enough in her life to know what she wants. I say, let's trust that she's going with her head and her instincts on this. We need to relax and let her live her life."

With her face flushed, Nora pressed her lips together and remained silent.

Douglas then looked at Rosa. "Okay, baby. We'll go with it the way you want us to. We'll be at Henri and Lenore's house later in the week, and we'll get them to take us to the club. We'll come as a group to hear you sing, and then we'll meet Louis, okay?"

"Okay. Thanks, Papa," Rosa said, beaming at her father.

*   *   *   *

Nora and Douglas had a joyous reunion with Henri and Lenore and Simone Monnier, Henri's mother. With Henri and Lenore they revisited Montmarte. Once they arrived, Douglas and Nora learned that the Le Deux and other nightclubs they remembered from long ago had closed and were replaced by different clubs. They rode with Henri and Lenore through various neighborhoods of Paris, and also revisited a couple of touristy landmarks, before spending some time in their friends' home.

Douglas and Nora and the Monniers did visit Chez Jolene and they enjoyed seeing Rosa perform. Much to Rosa's delight, they seemed to enjoy meeting Louis too. His charm obviously captivated them and his personality let them know he was compatible with Rosa. Douglas was confident and Nora seemed assured, after seeing and talking with Louis, that he was right for their daughter.

For the final couple of days of their two week visit to the City of Light, Nora and Douglas stayed with Rosa. When it was time for them to leave, Louis drove them to the airport. Rosa was in the passenger seat beside him.

Rosa was pleased that her parents now knew Louis, the man to whom she had pledged her love and with whom she had vowed to spend the rest of her life; which also meant she had decided to adopt Paris as her home.

She and Louis were going to visit them and the rest of the family, Rosa assured her father and mother. And Rosa would welcome her parents, Grandpa William, Willie and Dot and their spouses to visit her and Louis in Paris whenever they wanted to come.

Rosa believed her parents had come full circle. They had met and married in Paris. And as far as she knew, they had conceived her in Paris twenty-seven years ago. With their return to Paris to visit her, it was the three of them together in the City of Light again.

She was glad her parents lived long enough to see all their children grow up and become successful and happy with the life partners they had chosen. They did not have to worry about Willie, Dot or her again.

Rosa only wished Grandma Lilly were alive to see her eldest granddaughter's success. If only Grandma Lilly had lived long enough to learn that white Parisians and people of all colors and nationalities living in Paris loved her granddaughter's skin color and her artistry. And they made her feel at home.

Rosa now bloomed where she knew she was planted, and where she would continue to flower, not restricted under the cover of darkness but freely in the openness of light.

THE END

About the Author

A native of Washington, D.C., **Vee Garcia** majored in English and Literature at the University of the District of Columbia. Following a brief foray into magazine writing, she wrote fiction and saw a few of her short stories published. Soon she wrote longer works of fiction. Her earlier published novels include *Forbidden Circles* and *Whatever it Takes. The Jazz Flower* is her third novel. She is currently writing her fourth book. Vee Garcia lives in Florida with family and friends.

978-0-595-38174-6
0-595-38174-X

Printed in the United States
42442LVS00006B/76-102